On the Plus Side

ISBN 978-0-913123-40-9

First Published by Galileo Books in 2023

Book design by Adam Robinson
Back cover photograph by Photo by Tuân Nguyen Minh

FreeGalileo.com

ON THE PLUS SIDE

ASHLEY COWGER

For my little family: Max and Damien.
And for my furry BFFs:
Franny, Moonlight, Constantine, and Amity.
I love you all.

CON TENTS

HOW TO FIGURE THE RETURNS

E verything in life has a cost. It's Econ 101 stuff. Take me, for example. Take me and Keith. Moving in with him had its drawbacks, the most obvious being that I had to move all the way to Los Angeles, hundreds of miles away from my family and the internship—a *paid* one—that I'm pretty sure I would have been offered had I gone in for the interview. If I were to create a table to analyze that decision, it would include the move under the "Costs" column. There would be lots of other things too. Keith's nose whistled while he slept, and he always stacked his pomade in the medicine cabinet in such a way that it blocked my side of the cabinet from opening.

And there was Klepto. I hate dogs.

But there would be lots to put in the "Benefits" column, too. Things like the way he looked when he got home from work, all greasy and disheveled and sexy as hell, or the fact that he made enough money, I didn't technically need to work at all. I just did. I don't know why.

It's by weighing costs against benefits that you can determine something's true worth. You also have to consider how much value to give each item. The internship, say, should probably count more than how attractive I found Keith in his mechanic's coveralls. If I had gone to that interview, who knows where I'd be now? Not a waitress at Lollie's. I'd probably work longer, harder days, but I'd be working as an economist.

It's hard not to think about stuff like that when you're home sick on the couch, sitting in front of the TV and feeling insignificant. I was trying to distract myself from the return on investment of it all by watching a Hatha yoga tutorial. Sipping chicken broth from a mug and tilting my head this way and that as I watched a limber, skinny woman bend her body in impossible ways, I wondered whether I was just being paranoid or whether a four-days-late period was something to be concerned about. I had never been more than a day late in my life, and since I'd started on birth control when I was eighteen, my periods had been as predictable as dawn. So I was on the pill, and Keith smoked a bowl of weed every night to calm his nerves, which should have knocked down his sperm count. It seemed impossible that I might be pregnant, but it seemed equally impossible that I might not be. That's what I was thinking about—impossibilities, and whether I should suck it up and just take a test.

Klepto plopped himself down on the floor between the couch and the TV, right in front of me so I couldn't help but notice, and started doing his scratching thing. He'd been scratching impulsively—at his ears, behind his neck—and he'd rub his front legs down his face and let out a long, low whine that sounded like absolute agony. His dense, chocolate fur, which looked like ragged pieces of yarn to me, would whirl about his shaking body, and the rabies tag on his collar would jingle.

I walked over to the bathroom and leaned against the doorjamb. "Do you think Klepto might have fleas or something?" I asked Keith. My voice came out pinched and nervous, not at all how I had intended it. I cleared my throat and added, "I mean, just because he's been scratching so much lately."

Keith glanced at Klepto over his shoulder. "Nah. He's just itchy." He was standing in front of the mirror combing pomade into his dark brown hair. It's like he *wanted* to fit the stereotype of the oily mechanic, the way he dressed and did his hair and everything. Most days I liked it, but that day—I don't know. Something about the way his hair looked wet even though it wasn't, it kind of made my stomach churn. "Dogs get itchy, Rache. Just like people do," he said, double-checking his slicked back hair in the mirror.

I would have believed the scratching didn't mean anything if Klepto had always been an itchy sort of dog. He was a Standard Poodle, which is like a toy poodle blown up to the size of a Labrador, and his fur grew like brown tangles of human hair—thick and curly. But I'd been living with Keith for six years, and I'd never seen Klepto scratch like this before. Still, I knew better than to press it just then. I took another sip of my broth. "Maybe you're right."

After Keith headed to the shop that morning, Klepto tried to jump up on the couch and push his big, dumb head into my lap, but I pushed him off with my stockinged feet. "Get away from me, you disgusting thing," I said. He did his little whimper thing and gave me that same look he always did when I rejected his affections, but he left me alone and lay down on his doggy bed.

I spent the rest of the morning scouring the internet for information about fleas. How to know if your dog has them and how dogs get them, that sort of thing. Pretty soon I had filled a full page with notes. I didn't want to test Klepto for fleas myself—I didn't much like touching Klepto under normal circumstances—but I figured I could at least tell Keith what he needed to do.

I planned to tell Keith that it didn't do any good to pretend the problem away. I practiced saying it aloud to myself nine different ways. No matter how I worded it, though, I couldn't get the tone quite right. Keith knew I didn't really like Klepto. He would surely think I was just making more excuses for why we shouldn't own a dog.

I gave up on finding the right words and went upstairs to take a nap instead, but I couldn't really sleep. I kept hearing Klepto scratching on the floor beside the bed. I put my headphones in and pulled the blanket over my head, but it didn't help. I could still hear it: the jingling, the panting, the whines. I just lay there for hours, trying not to think, until I heard Keith opening the front door downstairs. By the time I'd pulled myself out of bed and went down, he'd already found the jotted notes about how to check for fleas. He was sitting at the table eating a sandwich and reading the notes when I walked in. He looked up.

"You're home early." I sat down on the floor, then thought about the flea larvae that might be slithering around in our high pile carpet. I stood up again and took a seat at the table, opposite Keith.

"Yeah," Keith said. "Nothing but oil changes today. They didn't need me." Keith shoved the last bite of his sandwich into his mouth and stood up. He picked up his plate and carried it into the kitchen, placed it in the sink. "How're you feeling?"

I shrugged. "The same."

He nodded, then walked back into the dining room and picked up my notes. "So you really think Klepto's got fleas, huh?"

I shrugged. "Couldn't hurt to check, right?"

He skimmed through the page. Then he called Klepto.

Klepto bounded over and put his forepaws on Keith's legs, knocking Keith back a step.

"That dog has no idea how big he is," I said.

"He's just being playful." Keith handed me the paper and bent down to rub Klepto behind the ears. "Aren't you, boy?"

I looked down at my notes. "You have to part his fur to get a look at the skin. If you see little black specks, like pieces of dirt, that means he's got them."

"Fleas look like pieces of dirt?"

"No. Their feces do."

He parted Klepto's fur and inspected the skin, then parted another patch and looked again. He let the fur go and rubbed it in tight circles. "But how do we know it's flea feces? It might just be dirt."

A cold heaviness formed in my stomach. "So that means you found some?"

He petted Klepto, looking down at him and not me. "I don't even know what I'm looking for, Rache." His voice had an edge to it.

I'm sure mine did too when I said, "I told you. Little black specks."

He sighed. "You can check if you're that concerned about it." He stood up and walked into the living room, Klepto trotting along behind him.

I hesitated, then followed. "He's *your* dog," I said, which sounded childish, I knew, but I didn't know what else to say. As nauseated as I'd already been feeling all day, the thought of touching Klepto's flea riddled fur just seemed like a bad idea.

"And *you're* the one who thinks he has fleas," Keith said.

"Fine." I reached down and roughly separated a patch of Klepto's fur and leaned down to get a better look. The tiny strip of white skin was speckled with black dirt. It looked exactly like the pictures I'd seen online. My stomach felt like it was giving out on me, and I ran down the hall and into the bathroom. I just barely made it to the toilet before I threw up.

The cost versus benefits of having a dog is a topic I'd given up broaching with Keith years before. I actually typed it all up in a spreadsheet for him once, and I let Keith decide the value for each item. Time spent walking the dog: -5, he said, because it was a hassle, true, but it was also kind of nice sometimes, didn't I think? Got us outside, forced us to exercise. Picking up your dog's warm shit: -20. Yeah, he agreed, that was the worst. The way the dog greets you with such enthusiasm when you get home: +10 (it had its drawbacks, I pointed out, when the dog weighs almost as much as you and can knock you over without meaning to). Snuggling with the dog in bed on a sluggish Sunday morning: +25.

It took us days to think of all the items that needed to go in one column or the other. We'd be sitting at dinner, and I'd throw out, "What about giving your dog a bath?" And he'd follow it up with, "Don't forget sweet, sloppy doggy kisses," which I thought should be a cost but he insisted was a benefit. The ultimate score, after we'd run out of items, was -1. We'd both insisted that we had won.

"The costs outweigh the benefits," I told Keith.

"By one," he said. "That's not statistically significant."

It took most of the day for Keith to finally accept that Klepto did have fleas, but he still didn't seem to think it was that big of a deal. "They're sucking his blood," I told Keith, and, "I don't want them sucking my blood too."

He thought I was making it seem worse than it was, but agreed to read through some articles about how to get rid of fleas. "Just as soon as you calm down," he said. "And stop scratching your legs. You're not covered in fleas."

I knew the flea thing shouldn't bother me. Fleas are common enough, and it probably made me seem petty and kind of prissy. But I didn't like the idea of something sucking my blood so it could grow big and strong. I had never liked the idea of a pet depending on me to begin with. But Keith had owned Klepto for something like ten years, and we'd been together, Keith and I, for just seven. Klepto had seniority.

When I'd found out that Keith had a dog, I didn't really mind the idea, thought it was kind of charming, even, but when we started talking about moving in together—me giving up my life back home to move to Los Angeles and start over with Keith—I was hesitant. But I loved Keith, and I loved that he wanted me to be right there. Loved that he'd never had another girlfriend living there with him. He wanted me to be the first. But as much as I loved him, I just couldn't bring myself to love that stupid dog. He was big and clumsy and tracked mud into the house. He barked at nothing half the time and smelled like mildewing hair clogging up a drain. Sometimes, when I'd get frustrated, I'd say something I didn't really mean to Keith, like, "If I had known you had a dog when we first met, I never would have responded to your DM," and Keith would cut back with something like, "If I had known you didn't like dogs, I never would have DMed you," but I knew he didn't really mean it, either.

Getting rid of fleas was a serious undertaking. You had to treat the animal, for starters, but also, you had to cleanse every possible spot in your house where flea eggs or flea larvae might be hiding. There was nothing we could really do about it that night, but suddenly the idea of lying down and wrapping myself in the blankets, resting my head on the pillow, seemed like a death wish. I don't know how I had managed it earlier. I didn't know what fleas looked like in real life—we hadn't actually seen any fleas on Klepto, just the signs of them, and the pictures of fleas online were all magnified—but I imagined the monsters themselves were too small to be noticed crawling around on black sheets.

When we climbed into bed, Klepto jumped onto our feet, like he always did, and I gasped and shooed him off. "Down!"

Klepto barked, then jumped back onto the bed, this time folding himself up solely on Keith's side.

Keith reached down and patted Klepto on the head. "It's okay, boy. Mama thinks you've got the plague."

"Don't call me mama," I said. "I wouldn't be that mutt's mom if you paid me."

Keith and Klepto locked eyes, and Keith shook his head. Klepto broke the eye contact to shift his weight to one side, tilt his head up, and scratch his neck. "Poor Klepto." Keith gave the dog another pat. "I bet those little buggies itch like hell, don't they?" Keith settled back into bed and rolled over, presenting his back to me.

I leaned my back against the headboard. Keith looked over his shoulder at me as I switched off the light. He lay his head back down, pretending not to notice that I wasn't lying down. I leaned against the headboard, sitting up, all night long. I barely slept at all, and when I did, I dreamed about parasites eating me alive.

The next morning, my period still hadn't come. I could tell before I even went into the bathroom, but I went in anyway and inspected my underwear. Then I gathered up everything in the house that was machine washable—curtains, pillow cases, rugs, all our clothes—and piled them inside the car to take to the laundromat. "Half that stuff isn't even dirty," Keith said when he woke up and saw that I had foraged through his side of the closet, but I just ignored him, and he shut up about it.

"I need you to pick up some flea treatment after work," I said.

"Okay," he said.

"And some flea bombs, for the apartment."

"Those things are toxic."

I grabbed my car keys. "Take Klepto with you to the shop tomorrow. By the time you get home, it'll be fine."

"Okay," he said. He looked at the keys in my hands. They were shaking. Then he stepped over to me and placed his palms on my shoulders. "Is everything okay?"

I nodded, stepping close to let his arms envelop me. I closed my eyes, but I had to pull back because I thought I might start to cry.

"It's just fleas. Dogs get fleas," he said. "It's nothing we can't handle."

I took up seven washers at the laundromat, and the old lady behind the desk gave me a disapproving look. The only other customer was some woman with two obnoxious, blond devils—twins, it seemed, probably like four or five. They were playing tag around the machines and hollering at each other: "You can't catch me!" I kept expecting the woman to say something to them, tell them to settle down or whatever it is that moms of little devils say, but she just stood there folding laundry and watching *Judge Judy* on the TV mounted to the wall.

After I had switched all the loads into the dryers, Celine, the manager at Lollie's, called. "Where are you?" No "Hey," or "How're you feeling?" or anything like that.

"At the laundromat."

She paused, then asked, "But why?"

I sighed. "There are flea eggs all over everything."

The lady behind the desk lifted an eyebrow at me. I turned my back to her.

"Okay. But do you have to do that now? Your shift started half an hour ago."

"I forgot."

"Forgot," she said, half under her breath.

"I don't have anything to wear." I watched the wet clothes whirl around and around in the dryer. One of the towels made a rhythmic thumping sound every time it hit the bottom. "And I'm still sick, anyway."

"Do you have the flu or something?" Celine asked.

"I'm not sure," I said. "Maybe."

"Well at least you could've called in."

"I think I may be sick, like, indefinitely."

"Indefinitely," she repeated.

"Yeah," I said. "Indefinitely."

"Wait, are you quitting?"

But just then, one of my dryers dinged, and I told her I had to go. Before she could protest, I hung up and set my phone to silent.

I popped the trunk to begin lugging the loads of clean laundry inside. Then it occurred to me that since Klepto and the house were still untreated, if I brought all this stuff in, it would just get contaminated again. I slammed the trunk closed.

The second I opened the front door, Klepto came barreling over, barking and panting and jumping up to press his dirty paws against my thighs. I swiveled around him and watched him topple to the ground. I snorted. "Serves you right."

He followed me into the kitchen, and just to get him off my back, I tossed him a couple of treats. Then I poured myself a bowl of cereal, walked to the living room, and sank into the sofa, perching the cereal bowl on my lap. Klepto trotted into the living room and lay down on his doggie bed, folding his paws in front of him and then dropping his head onto them, his eyes peering up at me.

I shook my head at him. "This isn't . . . I can't . . ."

Klepto lifted his head slightly, then dropped it back down and closed his eyes. I wanted to do the same, but I was sure there were microscopic beasts crawling all over the couch. Jumping. Fleas were supposed to be able to jump. I stared down at my cereal, then placed the bowl on the coffee table and drew my knees up to my chest. "Fuck," I said under my breath. Klepto's ears perked up, but he didn't open his eyes.

§

I spent the rest of the afternoon vacuuming the entire apartment. After I'd vacuumed everywhere I could reach, I moved all the furniture to the center of each room and vacuumed some more. When Keith came home and saw the state of the apartment and that I hadn't brought the laundry back in, he just kind of lifted one eyebrow at me but didn't say anything. His silence felt to me like an attack. "We can't just sit around and ignore them, Keith. They could kill Klepto." This last part didn't seem very likely, but I wanted Keith to feel guilty for his indifference.

"I don't think they're going to kill him," Keith said. The thing about Keith was that he was so fucking reasonable. It was irritating sometimes.

"But they could," I said.

"Hey," Keith said, stepping over to hug me. "It's okay, Rache. We'll get rid of them."

I pressed my face into his shoulder and breathed in the sweat and engine oil on his shirt. It was comforting, even though it smelled terrible. We just stood like that for a few minutes, my body quaking and his steadying it. Finally, I asked, "Did you get the flea bombs?"

"Yep," he said. "And the treatment for Klepto. I ran over to the vet during lunch."

I leaned in closer to him. "I can't bring the sheets and everything in until we've flea bombed the place," I said. "And I don't want to sleep here tonight."

Keith kissed the top of my head. "It's going to be okay."

I held Klepto steady as Keith administered the flea treatment—a tiny tube of goop that had to be squeezed onto the nape of Klepto's neck—then Keith took me out to dinner. When we got to the hotel, I dropped onto the bed and fell asleep.

§

When I woke up, it was dark outside, and Keith was gone. I felt disoriented and confused for a second until I found the note he'd left by the phone: "Went home to walk Klepto. Back in a bit." Then I remembered where I was and why.

I stripped off my clothes and climbed into the shower, turned the water up to just short of scalding and massaged the free hotel soap into my skin. All the articles we'd read said that getting rid of fleas could take months, that it's not uncommon for them to come right back a week or two after you think you've killed them all. The idea was exhausting, battling fleas for months to come, and all for a dog I hadn't even wanted to begin with.

But I did have a choice. I didn't have to live with fleas, or even with Klepto. With any of it. I could still get out. I could climb out of the shower, towel off and throw on my clothes, and I could check in to my own hotel room for the night. In the morning, I could head out. Move back home. The car was mine, and I already had it packed full of our laundry.

I rubbed my hands over my still taut belly and began to cry. I just stood there like that awhile—crying, the hot water reddening my skin. The bathroom door clicked. Keith's voice: "Don't freak out. It's just me."

I ran my face under the water to wash away any signs of tears.

Keith pulled back the shower curtain. "Get some good rest?" I nodded.

"You still look tired, though," he said, looking at my eyes.

I turned the water off. "Yeah," I said, wondering if he could tell I had been crying. Keith tossed me a towel, and I wrapped it around myself and climbed out. I wiped steam off the mirror. My eyes were puffy and red. "You know, if you want to go home and spend the night with Klepto."

Keith wrapped his arms around me from behind and kissed my neck. "Nah," he said. "I'll stay here with you. Unless," he added, looking at me through the mirror, "you'd rather be alone."

I stood there for a long few seconds, staring into the mirror's reflection of his eyes, and then I rested my head on his arm.

We made love that night in the sanitary hotel sheets, with no dog watching us from the foot of the bed. The next day, Keith took Klepto with him to the shop while I flea bombed the apartment. When they came home, Keith and I unloaded the laundry from the car and put the apartment back together. That night, after we climbed under the flea free blankets, I asked Keith if he thought we'd successfully killed all the fleas.

"I don't know how a single flea could have survived," he said.

"But they often come back a week or two later," I reminded him. "Do you think they might come back?"

He sighed and kissed me on the forehead. "I guess they might," he said. "And if they do, we'll get rid of them again."

"Yeah," I said, and nuzzled against his neck. "Hey, Keith?" I said, and for a second, I didn't know if I could say it. My heart seemed to stop beating; my hands shook. I had to close my eyes and force the words out.

"Really?" he asked. "For real?"

"For real," I said. "But before you get all excited, I should tell you I don't really know whether I want to have it."

There was a pause, and then he pulled me close. He didn't say anything after that.

THIRTY-EIGHT TODAY

Now there was pulsing on Marcia's chin. The pimple she'd felt forming under the surface the night before had erupted while she slept. She resisted the urge to touch it. She already knew what would be there: a soft, tender nodule which would surely look red and infected. She climbed out of bed and sat staring at her closed door.

I am thirty-eight today, she thought.

Her reflection in the streaky bathroom mirror confirmed her suspicion: the pimple was inflamed, almost the size of a dime at its base, and though she knew it was probably a trick of the light, it appeared to be visibly throbbing. After spending her teen years and most of her adulthood with severe, cystic acne, Marcia had believed she finally exchanged the need for all those drying acne treatments with the need for equally drying wrinkle creams. She didn't have benzoyl peroxide on hand, nor even concealer. Both facts would have seemed like a siren song to fate a few short years ago. She turned her chin up towards the mirror. *Thirty-eight*, she thought. When she walked into the kitchen fifteen minutes later, her face washed and her thin, blonde hair pulled into a tight knot, she thought about saying it out loud to her roommate, Dan: *I am thirty-eight today.*

Dan was rinsing out his coffee mug, a practice Marcia had always found unsanitary. It would take maybe thirty extra seconds to actually wash it with soap and a sponge, but Dan seemed to believe a quick rinse was sufficient. Were Dan and Marcia in a romantic relationship, Marcia would say something. As it was, Marcia didn't feel it was her place, so instead of speaking up, she surreptitiously washed Dan's coffee mug for him once a week or so, after he'd gone to work.

She watched Dan shake droplets of water from his mug before placing it upside down in the dish drain. She thought again about saying the words: "Today, I am thirty-eight," or maybe even just, "It's my birthday." Instead, she asked him, "Want to have lunch?"

"Can't." He wiped the excess water from his hands on the front of his pants. *Jesus, Dan,* she thought, *there's a towel right there.* "Having lunch with a client."

"Oh," she said. "Maybe dinner, then."

"Maybe," he said.

After Dan left for work, Marcia poured herself a bowl of cereal and ate it slowly, staring at the kitchen wall. Why hadn't she just told him it was her birthday? Better yet, why hadn't she told him days ago, when the big day was still on the horizon? It's not like she hadn't been thinking about it, been wondering whether Dan might remember, might get her a present, surprise her with a pineapple upside down cake. They'd known each other for four years now. It was long enough to remember each other's birthday, each other's favorite dessert. Marcia knew it was long enough, because she remembered Dan's: March 28th, chocolate swirl ice cream cake.

Her life would have been different had she and Dan both been single when they'd met. It was something she thought about often. Would they have begun dating instead of initiating a clumsy friendship? Would he remember her birthday now? Things between them had seemed only to get more awkward when both Marcia and Dan had found themselves single a week apart. They'd both taken up residence in an extended-stay motel, by sheer coincidence just four doors apart. It had made sense, they agreed, to find an apartment together, and after that it had seemed ever less likely that anything beyond an arm's length friendship might develop between the two of them. Marcia assumed Dan didn't think it would be a good idea, roommates sleeping together.

Marcia stood up to wash her cereal bowl. *I am not in love with my roommate*, she told herself, and it was true: she wasn't. Still, sometimes she had to remind herself. Like when Dan would surprise her with his lasagna, just when she felt she would rather starve than make dinner, or when she'd notice him noticing another woman and feel an unexpected flush rise to her cheeks.

But she didn't love him, not in the romantic sense. He'd become a close friend over the years, it was true, but it was a kind of closeness based on proximity more than anything. They didn't tell each other personal things, knew very little about each other's pasts. When Dan's parents came to visit, they stayed at a hotel, and if they'd ever stopped by to see the apartment, they'd done so when Marcia had been at work. She hadn't met them.

Marcia's sister had flown in for the weekend once. Dan introduced himself simply as "the roommate" before absenting himself from the apartment for the majority of Cynthia's stay.

Still, Dan was the only person Marcia felt any real connection to anymore. She was glad that both their relationships had fallen apart when they did. She was glad that, in her late thirties, with no pets and no lovers and a brittle connection to her family, she had someone to sit and watch Netflix with at the end of the day.

On her way to the bus, Marcia allowed herself to daydream about a birthday surprise. What if Dan was only pretending not to know? What if he'd bought her some cupcakes—no, tulips, thirty-eight of them—and had ordered them delivered to Marcia's office? She knew it was farfetched, so she only let herself think about it for the four blocks it took to get to the bus stop.

The bus was abnormally crowded. She scanned the seats searching for a vacancy. A woman near the back lifted her hand in the air. "There's a spot right here."

Marcia paused when she reached the back and saw that the woman, who was shifting an overstuffed canvas bag from the vacant seat onto the floor, held in her lap a fat, drooling baby. Marcia glanced around the bus again, hoping there might be another empty seat she'd missed, but the bus lurched forward and Marcia pitched back, then stumbled into the seat.

"Don't worry," the woman told Marcia. "He doesn't bite.'

The baby watched Marcia with red, puffy eyes. Marcia smiled at him, and he twisted around and buried his face in his mother's shirt.

"Shh," the woman said softly, stroking the baby's wispy hair. "It's okay."

"I guess I make him nervous," Marcia said.

"He's just coming into that anxiety stage," the woman said.

"I think I'm still in that stage myself," Marcia said, but the woman didn't laugh.

Marcia swiped her phone on and opened Facebook. She knew she could count on, if nothing else, a birthday wish from her mom there. When she'd gone to college, her mom had called on her birthday, but over time the calls had turned into texts. Now, her mom wrote a message on her Facebook wall, sometimes accompanied with a GIF of a kitten pouncing onto a birthday cake, or a cartoon frog dancing in a party hat.

There it was: happy birthday sweetie

All lower case and no punctuation, as if Marcia wasn't worth the time it took to hit the extra keys. There were eleven other posts too, all saying variations of the same thing. Twelve birthday wishes total, but it was still morning yet.

Marcia slid her phone into her purse and tilted her chin toward the baby. "How old is he?"

"Six months."

The baby turned his head again and stared at Marcia. He had intense, blue eyes and round, chapped cheeks. Marcia waved at him. He looked from her hands back to her face, then reached out and grasped onto her pimple. Marcia winced.

The woman batted the baby's hand away. "Nononononononono. We don't . . . no." The woman avoided eye contact with Marcia as she said, "I'm so sorry."

The pain had caused Marcia's eyes to water, but she quickly brushed the wetness away. "It's fine. He's just exploring." She looked at the baby and said in a lulling tone, "It's just a pimple, isn't that right? People get pimples sometimes."

The woman reached into her bag and rummaged inside with one hand until she pulled out a rattle. The baby's eyes widened and his mouth gaped open into a broad grin as the woman gave the rattle a fierce shake then pressed it into his tiny hands. He squealed, then brought the rattle to his mouth and began to suck noisily.

Marcia watched the whole scene with detached curiosity— that such a tiny, inconsequential gift could make the boy's eyes light up so. The baby saw her watching and pulled the rattle out of his mouth long enough to blow a raspberry in her direction.

"Ah-boo," the mother mimicked, repositioning the baby's weight on her lap.

"Ah-boooooooooo," the baby said, eyes still locked on Marcia's.

"He wants you to do it back to him," the mother said.

"Ah-boooooooooo," the baby said, holding out his rattle and deliberately dropping it on the floor.

"Ah-boo," Marcia said.

The baby squealed.

Marcia picked up the rattle and shook it at the baby.

"He likes you," the mother said. "You must be a good person. He can tell."

Marcia was half-expecting a surprise birthday card or a cake at the office. Something. Some of her coworkers were "friends" on Facebook. Maybe somebody had noticed. If they had, nobody said anything, and Marcia made her way to her desk with little more than the ordinary "Morning" and "How's it going?" Her focus kept drifting from the forms it was her job to check and double check. She kept finding herself compelled to pull up Facebook to see if anyone else had wished her a happy birthday. She couldn't explain it, but she felt sure that any minute, Dan would post, or somebody interesting. She had a strange, expectant feeling in her stomach, some kind of psychic energy, she thought, not that she really believed in that sort of thing. Still, it was her birthday, and the baby on the bus had deemed her worthy of his rattle.

That fat-cheeked, bubble-blowing baby—so ugly, the way all babies are when you don't have any connection to them or their parents. Someone had once told Marcia that children can see into your soul. They see things adults miss, pick up on cues, so when a child likes you, it means more than when a grown-up does. Plus, children love selflessly and without fear of the consequences. A child can love purely, solely because you make him laugh, or because your grilled cheese sandwiches are the gooiest. They cut to the heart of things, kids. They don't get caught up in your mistakes.

When she was a child herself, Marcia had believed she would have a baby of her own one day. It wasn't so much a desire as an assumption. When the time was right, when she settled down, when she married and bought a home. But none of those prerequisites had gotten around to happening, and now, at thirty-eight, she understood without ever having consciously realized it, it was probably too late. She didn't feel she had missed out on some great adventure by not having a child, and it wasn't like the opportunity had never presented itself. It wasn't like she regretted not taking the chance when she had it. It was just the framework of it all, the pimple and the birthday and the lack of anyone actually saying the words, "Happy birthday. I'm glad you're alive." That and the fact that the baby somehow knew she was good.

Marcia took herself out for a birthday lunch at the mall. When she'd been in her twenties, she'd gotten herself into trouble with credit card debt and, ever since she'd rebuilt her credit score to something passable, she tried her best to avoid the mall. But it was, after all, her birthday, and there was a strange sort of pleasure in the garbage only mall food courts could get away with serving.

The noodles were greasy and delicious, the Cinnabon, a giant, 800-calorie piece of heaven. Marcia ate deliberately, chewing slowly to make the calories count. After lunch, she followed the vibrant yellow signs indicating the mall walkers' lap. She told herself she was doing it to burn off some of the calories she'd just consumed. She walked by the Victoria's Secret without giving it a second glance, even passed by Elder Beerman. She fought the urge to pop into the Hallmark store—she was a sucker for Itty Bitties—but she checked the time on her phone and convinced herself not to waste any of her five remaining minutes before she had to head back to the office.

Her eyes were drawn to something shiny at a nearby jewelry kiosk: a golden bangle with a large, emerald-colored heart dangling from its center. It reminded her of the bangles her grandmother used to wear. Marcia remembered the coziness of Nana's living room, Nana's mildly rose-scented skin. Marcia used to sit on Nana's lap as they watched reruns of *Lawrence Welk*, Nana's fingers smoothing Marcia's hair, her bangles clicking softly against each other. Tingles would spread from somewhere inside Marcia's brain outward, and she never knew if it was the sound of the bangles or the feeling of Nana's gentle strokes that caused it, but nothing in her life had ever given her such pleasure again.

"Lovely, isn't it?" the woman working the booth asked when she noticed Marcia eyeing the bangle.

"Oh. Yes. It's nice." Marcia started to walk away.

"Looking for yourself or as a gift?"

Marcia forced a smile. "A birthday present, I guess. I mean, neither, really. Just killing time."

"Well, just so you know, everything is 20% off right now."

"Oh really?" Marcia looked back at the bangle. The heart sparkled beneath the mall's skylight.

"You came at a good time. Sale ends today."

"How much is it at 20% off?" Marcia asked.

Marcia recognized the look on the woman's face. It was the salesperson look of victory. "Only $125. Or you can get three bangles for $300."

It wasn't as though Marcia had that much disposable income. $300 was a lot to Marcia. Still, Marcia left with the bangle, and two others, encrusted with tiny crystals, to wear with it, which the woman closed inside a gift box with a bow. Marcia thought about waiting to open the box, dangling it in front of herself as a sort of carrot to get her through the day, but as soon as she stepped through the mall's double doors, she untied the bow and slid the box open. She slid the bangles onto her wrist and admired the way their golden curvature enhanced her slender features. Her whole arm looked prettier, she thought, even her hand. Her fingers, which she often worried were too bony, witch-like, seemed delicate and elegant. She thought she might even have her nails done after work—a French manicure. Why not?

As she walked back to the office, she noticed the faint clicking as the bangles rattled against each other. It was like a subtle drumbeat turning the meaningless muddle of traffic sounds into music. She had an inkling that she was meant to find these bangles, that fate was at play, although she couldn't say why purchasing some overpriced jewelry should be so important. Maybe the purchase was significant because it was a sign of how far she'd come, the distance she'd put between her past and today. In fact, it was almost hard to believe, sometimes, that she was the same person she'd once been. When she was with the boyfriend before the one she was living with when she met Dan, she'd been so passive, so submissive and unsure. On nights when he stayed out late drinking, she'd fall asleep with the bed and blankets to herself, then wake up to him on top of her. Rather than getting into another fight, she'd pretend to be asleep until he finished, until he grunted in his unappealing way and rolled off of her, falling almost immediately to sleep. Then she'd creep into the bathroom to clean herself off.

That was so long ago now, back in Arizona, back before she'd packed up and moved, without leaving a note. He'd shown up on her mom's doorstep looking for her, and that was how her family found out she was gone. It was weeks before she'd gotten in touch with her sister, told her she was fine, she'd found a place and a job and everything. She didn't tell her she had already moved in with a new boyfriend, that she'd remained single for all of six days before rushing, head-first, into what would prove to be a four-year-long rebound relationship. And now, here she was, walking back to work, expensive jewelry hanging from her wrist, which she had bought as a birthday present for herself, thank you very much. It *did* mean something, didn't it? It had to.

Marcia half-expected somebody to notice the bangles, or to at least notice that something seemed different, but nobody did. She knew she shouldn't be, but she was disappointed. The crystals didn't sparkle in the fluorescent light the way they had in the sunlight, but still, these bracelets *were* lovely, just like the sales lady had said. It seemed strange that nobody, not even Jane in accounting, who always wore the most ostentatious jewelry, would notice. Still, she tried not to let it bother her, tried to focus on work.

At 3:00, during her weekly meeting with her supervisor, Marcia found herself gesturing flamboyantly as she spoke, trying to draw Sheryl's attention to her wrist. At one point, Sheryl's eyes rested for what seemed to Marcia a prolonged amount of time on the bangles before flitting away again. When the meeting was over and Sheryl reached out to grasp Marcia's wrist, just above the bracelets, Marcia thought, *at last.*

"Marsh," Sheryl said, in a hushed voice, even though her office door was closed and nobody else was in the room. "Can I give you my dermatologist's name? He's a miracle worker."

Marcia's cheeks grew warm. "Oh," she said. "Okay."

"Just from one woman to another," Sheryl said as she jotted the name on a Post-it. She handed it to Marcia. "I have terrible rosacea, but you'd never know to look at me."

"Thanks." The blue ink blurred against the yellow background as she stared at the note. "I'll look him up."

"Do it," Sheryl said.

"Thanks," Marcia said again.

And it was then, as she walked back to her desk, that the clicking started to get to her. That clicking—more of a clanking, really—it was so loud, or was it just that the office around her was so quiet? All she could hear was the murmur of voices in the conference room, the gentle clacking of fingers skating across keyboards, and the tick, tick, tick of her bangles, every time she moved.

She listened to the clicking until 5:00. She listened to it on the bus; she listened to it mingle with her footfall on the walk from the bus stop to her apartment. She listened to it as she sat at the table, waiting for Dan, wondering if they might have dinner together, if he might have figured out about her birthday. She took off the bracelets, laid them on the table in front of her, and poured herself a glass of wine. Under the bright white LED kitchen light, the crystals looked dull. The bangles were still pretty, dainty and sweet, but not worth $300. She wasn't even sure the heart was a genuine emerald. It looked like it may be made of glass. Marcia wondered if there really had been a sale that ended today. Didn't mall kiosks run perpetual sales? Perhaps tomorrow, a new sale would have started, a better sale. Perhaps her stumbling upon the bangles wasn't the kismet it had felt like in the moment.

Before she'd left Arizona, the man before the man before Dan had given her a promise ring, or at least, that's what he'd called it. Not an engagement ring, he'd said, but a promise to become engaged. When he was ready, he'd said. When he'd had a chance to finish growing up. He'd told her it was expensive, that it was a genuine diamond, but she'd known, even with her limited experience with authentic gemstones, that it was a fake. She didn't tell him that she knew, or that she didn't want to put it on because the thought of wearing it made her feel hopeless, even more hopeless than she'd felt when her period had been eight days late. At least then, it had been a sort of secret, a secret she could control. And it wasn't that she'd ever made the decision to get rid of the baby or anything like that. She hadn't even made the decision to take a pregnancy test. That, like wearing the ring, would have felt too final. There was freedom in the not-knowing. There was freedom in the fact she could walk all day in the dry, Tucson heat. She could walk until she had blisters on her feet and her left sock had sprung a hole, and that night, when she saw the blood on her underwear, she could know that she wasn't trapped, after all, and that she would never know if she'd even been pregnant, not for sure, and that it didn't matter anyway because she wasn't now, nor would she ever let herself be, not by this man.

This emerald, she suddenly felt certain, just like that diamond, wasn't real. Marcia drained the last of her wine glass in one gulp and refilled it with the remainder of the bottle. Then, without thinking, really, without deciding to do it, she brought the bottom of the bottle down, hard, atop the emerald heart. She lifted the bottle up and brought it down again, this time even harder. The heart crunched beneath the weight. She slid the bottle to the center of the table and sat, silently sipping the rest of her wine. When Dan came home, that's where he found her: alone at the table, in front of a spent bottle of wine and a stack of bent and broken bangles, coated in green dust.

"Everything okay?" he asked. He rubbed the palm of his right hand over his head, which Marcia knew meant he was anxious.

"Fine," she said carefully, trying not to slur.

"What happened to your bracelets?" He picked them up. Dislodged crystals pattered against the table.

She shrugged. "They broke."

"No doubt." He pulled a chair up and inspected what was left of the bangles.

"It was a birthday present," Marcia said.

He looked up, one eyebrow raised. "Shit. It's your birthday." It wasn't a question, which she appreciated. He said it like it was something he should have known. "They came in the mail like this?"

She nodded.

"Fucking post office." He rubbed his head again. "Maybe the package was insured?"

Marcia shook her head.

"Fuck. I'm sorry." He placed the bangles back on the table gently, as though any further harm could come to them now.

"It's okay." She laughed. "It's kind of funny, really."

He shook his head. "I'm sorry I didn't get you anything. Or remember." He picked up the wine bottle and shook it. "Happy birthday."

"Thanks."

He leaned back in the chair and turned the empty bottle around and around in his hands.

"I'm thirty-eight today," she told him.

"I know."

No, you don't, she wanted to say. "Some baby on the bus thinks I'm a good person," she said instead.

"Oh?" This time both eyebrows raised. He looked ridiculous. She laughed. "Have a glass of wine with me," she said.

He shook the empty bottle again and looked at her, his head cocked. He placed the bottle on the table. "Maybe a glass of water instead."

"I'm not that drunk," she said, and as if on cue, the world around her began to spin.

He leaned forward and squeezed her forearm—a quick, gentle pressure, and then his hand was gone, but the warmth of his skin lingered.

"I'm okay." The words bled together, and she felt suddenly overcome with fatigue. "I'm going to be okay."

BETTER DAYS

My sister Kayla's suicide note took the form of a Tweet. Someone, I can't remember who, took it as a joke—well, because how else are you supposed to take something like that? They tweeted back: "The way you choose to kill yourself says more about you than just about anything." Kayla used a kitchen knife, which she cleaned, for some reason, with bleach, before she ran it down her forearm several times. Despite the antiseptic smell that mingled with her blood, it was a messier death than I would have expected of Kayla, who was always the neat twin, the polite one.

That was really how it all began: the compulsion, if you want to call it that. I like to call it my OCD shining through, because everybody you've ever met claims to be "a little" OCD, so I don't see why I shouldn't, too. It started as a result of Kayla's death, or anyway, a result of the time I got to spend reflecting on life and death—especially the self-inflicted kind—as I lay awake in our shared childhood room. It gave me time to think. About all those things you tell yourself you'll think about when you have time, which is pretty much never when you're a sopho-more in college and your English professor thinks you should write twelve drafts of every paper, and your Psychology professor seems to think that his is the only class you're taking.

I thought about blood, and how it looks different on the outside of your body than the in. And about life. It's short when you stop and add it all up. It feels like just yesterday Kayla and I were eight years old, swinging on the swingset in the backyard—Kayla going higher and higher, me screaming, "No, Kayla. You'll fall!"

And I thought about death, of course, about how it can come unexpectedly, and yet in Kayla's case we were warned. We were all warned. Because I saw that Tweet when I was at the library. She'd tagged me in it: @KylieGrrl98. I don't know why. I saw it and put off coming home for two more hours. But what got me, what kept clanging around inside my head as I stared at the glow-in-the-dark stars Kayla had arranged as constellations on our ceiling, was that Kayla had given *herself* fair warning too. We all die, sooner or later, and only the most delusional of us try to pretend that away, but Kayla got to say when and how.

I don't want you to think that I'm some kind of apathetic bitch. She was my sister, after all, my twin. I loved her. I thought about the other things, too. The regular things. Wondered why she did it and how long she'd been feeling this way. If there was anything I could have done. But there was no way I could ever know the answers to those questions. Kayla had been the one with the mind for abstract thought. I was more interested in the facts: the who, what, when, where, why, and how of it all. And the first fact was that we all die. The second fact was that if we don't choose when and how, some force outside of ourselves— fate, if you want to call it that—chooses for us.

And the third fact was that Kayla had chosen for herself.

Kayla and I used to trick people by pretending to be each other. It worked on almost everybody—our Sunday School teachers, our friends, even our aunts and uncles. When Aunt Cara picked us up at the bus stop sometimes, she used to say out loud what color shirt each of us was wearing: Kayla, red; Kylie, purple. Then, we'd switch shirts in her bathroom, and she'd call me Kayla and Kayla, me. She'd ask me questions about Math club, and Kayla would try not to laugh as I made up fake equations. Our mom was the only one who could always tell the difference. She said we had distinct facial expressions and Kayla's voice was gentler, her eyes always opened a little bit wider.

I never thought we looked exactly alike. My hair was frizzier than Kayla's, so even when we'd style it the same, hers looked smoother. Her chin was set slightly higher than mine, too, more upturned. I used to look at her and try to see myself. We came from one egg that had split into two. That separation marks you for life. They say twins have a sort of metaphysical connection, that they can feel each other's pain. When we were eleven, I pricked my index finger to see if Kayla could feel it. I blindfolded her, so she wouldn't know when the pin entered my skin, and asked her to tell me the moment she felt the sting. I pressed the pin in slowly, watching as my skin ballooned around it before giving into the pressure. Kayla said, "Ouch," but I couldn't tell if she really felt it or not. When we reversed the roles—Kayla pressing the pin into her forearm this time, so my already sore finger wouldn't invalidate the experiment—I lied and said I could feel it.

My first night back at the apartment after Kayla's death, after the funeral and the procession of well-meaning but distant relatives and family friends who patted me on the back or squeezed my shoulders and told me how sorry they were, or how much I reminded them of Kayla, or what a beautiful soul she'd had, I didn't sleep. I closed my eyes and just lay there, watching suicide on parade. Kayla was acting out all the different ways there are to kill yourself. I knew it was fucked up, imagining my sister killing herself in any and every crazy way I could think of, but I couldn't stop the images from coming: Kayla mixing drain cleaner with her morning coffee. Kayla slowly taking the stairs to the top floor of the library and then going through that door in the back corner—the one with the sign that says Emergency Exit, even though it couldn't possibly be, why would they put an Emergency Exit that leads out onto the roof?—and jumping. Her long, brown Medusa curls slithering through the air. The crunch when her body hit the cement.

I opened my eyes and rolled over. The nightmare images of Kayla killing herself stopped, but then my mind just started thumbing through the different ways there are to kill yourself—overdosing on Tylenol, drinking poison, choking myself with a jump rope—like I was trying to commit a grocery list to memory. If Kayla were alive, I would have gone into her room and woken her up, told her we should make some popcorn and watch a movie, or I would just ask her to make me laugh. She could always make me laugh on cue.

The next morning, I climbed out of bed and went to the bathroom to brush my teeth, and when I stuck the toothbrush in my mouth, I had this impulse to push it all the way down my throat, just jam it down there and watch myself in the mirror as my eyes widened and bulged. I pulled the toothbrush out again and stared down at it. My hand shook. Even holding the toothbrush at sink level, I could still see it all clearly in my mind—me pushing the toothbrush so far down I couldn't pull it back out again, watching my own face redden, then go blue.

The impulses kept coming. I'd be at work and imagine plunging my face into the Fryolator. I'd see an empty nail sticking out of a wall and think about banging my forehead against it repeatedly, until the nail tore through my skull and pressed into my brain. It was weird, because it wasn't like I actually wanted to kill myself. I wasn't really depressed. I mean, I missed Kayla, yeah, of course I missed Kayla. She was the only one who knew that I could only fall asleep listening to true crime ASMR, the only one who shared my obsession with revenge horror movies. You don't lose someone that close to you and not feel it, you know, hard. But depression, to me, seems like a deep, low down kind of feeling. Like you cry a lot and feel a lot of pain. I didn't feel like that. I felt more, I don't know, tired.

Despite the violent impulses, I kept on doing all the things a person in my position was supposed to do. I emailed all my teachers and explained the situation to them, I guess expecting a little leeway, even though I hadn't really been a star student before my "emotional distress." I even went to talk to the school counselor, at the request of both my Anatomy professor and my mom. The counselor asked me all kinds of inane questions about whether I felt angry at Kayla and whether I blamed myself. I answered honestly—yes, I guessed I felt a little angry; no, I didn't really blame myself. When she asked me if I ever thought about killing myself, I quickly told her no.

I only went to the counselor a couple of times, and I stopped going to my classes altogether, but I kept going to work. The knives made me nervous, but otherwise it seemed like the safest place for me to be. Sometimes I'd get so busy, I didn't really have time to think about the urges. I didn't have time to think about anything, and that suited me just fine. I told my boss I would probably be dropping out of school, so if he needed me for extra hours, that would be fine. He said he'd keep me in mind for when people called in sick or whatever. It wasn't really what I was hoping he'd say, because sitting around the apartment by myself was starting to get to me.

See, even though I didn't like it, I'd started to think of the compulsion as kind of a game. I realized that however you kill yourself is really like your last chance to speak before people put words in your mouth for the rest of eternity. However you do it, that's the first thing that will come to everybody's mind whenever they think of you. Kayla Trubright? Oh, she's that girl who slit her wrists. Her blood made purple pools on the wood floor. I think of that before I think of her laugh, or how she used to tug on her lower lip when she was nervous. The compulsion seemed like kind of a test run. If I *were* to do it, how would I go about it? What message would I want to send?

Without even meaning to, I'd begun a running list of the various ways of committing suicide I'd thought about so far and how each way might be perceived. Downing a cup of broken glass would be like saying, "Hey, world, fuck you." Whereas something less painful, say overdosing on sleeping pills, would be more like saying, "I'm sorry. I just can't take it anymore." Kind of wimpy, if you ask me. I mean, if you're going to do it, *do* it, you know what I mean?

What slitting your wrists meant, I couldn't decide. Had Kayla been trying to tell us she was sorry, or was she flipping off the entire world? It seemed like a painful death, but a quiet sort of painful, and she did it in the privacy of our own apartment. I couldn't quite put my finger on what she'd been trying to say, and for some reason, that really bothered me. It felt important, her final message. Felt like, after what she'd put herself through to send it, we should all try our best to decode it, to listen.

A few weeks after Kayla's death, I got a phone call from Student Services. "Every single one of your professors," he told me, "has filled out an academic intervention form for you."

I told him about Kayla and how the school counselor had told me I shouldn't push myself too hard with school right now if I didn't feel I could handle it, which was true.

He said that was alright, but I should know that it was too late to drop my classes, and if I didn't work something out with my professors so I could get deferrals and finish the classes out later, I would end up with a bunch of F's on my transcripts, and that would mean I'd be on academic probation. His voice was brusque, and he seemed like he was in a rush, as if I was the one who had called to bother him.

"Thanks for letting me know," I told him and hung up before he had a chance to say anything—you're welcome, probably, because he probably didn't even notice I was being sarcastic.

I thought about calling my mom and telling her I was dropping out, but she was helping out with Kayla's half of the rent. Plus, she was sending me supplemental money on the side to help cover the holes my part-time salary left behind. If I dropped out of school, she would cut me off, emotional distress or no, so instead, I went in to talk to my professors and asked them about getting a deferral. My Spanish professor said he would have been happy to help me if I hadn't already missed so many classes prior to "the incident," but everyone else said we could work something out. My Journalism professor even said if I still completed the final paper, an investigative report, I might pass the class with a C, depending on how well I did.

I didn't really feel like writing an investigative report, but I didn't want to end up on the streets because I couldn't make rent, either, so I told her I would do the best I could. The question was, what the fuck was I going to investigate? Professor Tilden gave me a bunch of possible topics: issues relating to the local economy, politics. I heard myself ask her if I could do something a bit more personal, like suicide rates in our area.

"That could work," she said. "Only, I don't want you to take on a topic that's going to be," she paused, "overtly . . . stressful. For you."

"It'll be fine," I said. "I was just thinking I'd interview someone at the suicide hotline or something." I'd seen this big, hand written, poster board sign for the suicide hotline nailed to the oak tree outside the Liberal Arts building: "Feeling lost? We can HELP! Better days ahead!"

"That sounds like a great place to start," Professor Tilden told me.

§

The place where they answered the phones was cramped and stuffy, just one long room with cubicle walls partitioning one desk off from the next. Brent, who was the Managing Volunteer, showed me around before I interviewed him. It was depressing, actually seeing the volunteers—my age, most of them, or not much older—sitting around at these cubicles talking earnestly on the phone, taking notes. "We keep detailed records of each phone call," Brent told me. He had those big, circular glasses that nerds always wear on TV, the kind you expect no real person to buy. On top of that, he was overweight, not obese or anything, but his face was circular and soft, and I wondered if he ever got made fun of at school and if he had many friends.

"And over here," he told me, pointing to a bulletin board with letters and printed emails tacked to it, "is where we post letters we receive from past callers, thanking us for helping them.

I glanced over the pages pinned to the board. "There aren't that many."

"Well, for every hundred people we save, probably only one writes to say thank you. If that many."

"So how do you know you saved all one hundred then?" I asked.

"They called, didn't they? They reached out for help. People who reach out for help almost never end up killing themselves in the end."

If the people who end up calling are not the ones who end up killing themselves, what good was the suicide hotline doing anyone, I wanted to ask. Kayla would never have called a suicide hotline. I was sure of it. She never so much as mentioned to *me*, her closest friend in the whole world, that she was feeling a little down. Who were these people who called suicide hotlines, I wondered, and why did they do it? What did they hope to gain?

Brent led me into his tiny square of an office and motioned for me to sit in the stiff, foldout chair across from his desk. I pulled out my portable audio recorder and placed it on the desk between us, then pressed the red button. My mom had given me the recorder when I graduated from high school; she said all journalists need something like this, but I hardly ever used it. Why would I need to? I had a phone.

I told Brent again what I was writing about and asked him why he thought suicide rates were so high in our area.

Brent told me, "College towns invariably have a lot of potential suicides, or just people who need to reach out to someone who will listen."

"Why do you think that is?" I asked.

"Stress. From school, from romantic relationships, from trouble with their parents, from being on their own for the first time. It's a hard time in any kid's life."

I pursed my lips, wondering how old he was that he was referring to me and Kayla and people like us as "kids," but I let it drop. "Can I ask," I said, "have you ever thought about suicide? Or is that too personal?"

"I think most people have thought about it to some extent or other, don't you?"

"But seriously, though. Like where you're planning out how you might go about it," I said.

"No," he said—too quickly, I thought. "I've never seriously thought about it."

I glanced down at my notebook, where I'd scribbled some half-formed questions a few minutes before the interview. "Can you walk me through a typical call? What do the callers usually say, and how do the operators respond?"

Brent leaned back in his seat. "Well, of course every call is unique, just like every caller."

"Do they ever, like, tell you how they're planning on doing it or anything like that?"

He shrugged. "Most of them haven't gotten that far in the planning process. Like I said, most of them aren't really going to do it. Their calling us is a cry for help."

I looked down at my questions, which all seemed pointless now that I knew that most of the people calling weren't the real suicidal people anyway. This whole interview seemed like it was going to be a bust unless I thought of some way to salvage it. I tapped my pen against my notebook. "Let's say," I said, looking up at the ceiling. "Let's say someone calls and tells you she can't stop thinking about killing herself. She doesn't *want* to kill herself, but she thinks about it, like, constantly. What would you tell her? How would you answer that cry for help?"

He folded his arms and looked up at the ceiling too. "Well," he said, "I'd probably start by telling her she did the right thing by calling. It's important to encourage them," he said, now looking at me. "Let them know that they *are* taking the right steps, that there *is* something we can do to help."

I fought the urge to roll my eyes. "Okay, but like, then what would you say? How are you going to keep her from actually going through with it?"

"It doesn't sound like she wants to go through with it, which is a great place to start. I'd probably talk to her about the feelings she's been having, ask her when they come on and how she handles them, if she's ever attempted to act on them, that sort of thing."

"Let's say she tells you they come on randomly, several times a day. She's never tried to act on them, but when they hit her, she feels like she has to hold herself back or she might do it. Let's say she tells you she's afraid she might actually do it one of these days, even though she doesn't want to."

"I'd ask her to tell me a little about herself. What's her life like? Is everything going okay at school? Is she in a romantic relationship, and if so, is it a happy one? Has she been having problems with her friends or with her parents? That kind of thing.

Usually, it doesn't take long to get at the heart of the problem. Usually there's some stimulus, something that's bothering the person and making them feel hopeless.'"

"What if there isn't?"

"There usually is."

"But let's say this time, there isn't. Everything's fine. Nothing's going wrong. She just wonders, sometimes, you know," but I stopped. Suddenly, my mouth felt full of saliva, and I didn't want to but I had to swallow before I could say anything more. "Like, what's the point?"

He stared at me for a few long seconds, then sucked in his breath. "To be honest," he told me, "I'd probably recommend she seek professional help."

I headed straight home after the interview with my portable audio recorder propped up in my lap so I could listen to the muffled recording. As I drove, I listened closely to my voice. It sounded different than how it had sounded in my head. It was hesitant, kind of unsure of itself, maybe even pleading. I'd thought I'd been poised, sort of stern during the interview. I thought I'd had a wry, cynical undertone. This person on the recording sounded like someone other than me.

The interview was a total waste, I decided. I thought about emailing Professor Tilden and backing out, just taking the F and being done with it—who cares? Writing this report was pointless. Finishing school was pointless, too. If the Hot Dog Shack didn't have full-time hours to offer me, maybe I'd take a second job somewhere else, or just quit, move, start over somewhere new. I'd tell my mom to go fuck herself; if she thought a college education was so important, she could get one. I had better things to do.

Except that I didn't, really. Have better things to do.

The interview ended with me thanking Brent for his time, followed by the sound of me picking the recorder up and turning it off. I reached down to press stop, but before I pressed the button, Kayla's voice came on, in mid-sentence. At first I thought this was some sort of suicide note. My cheeks flushed. But then my voice came on, and I remembered what it was. I'd forgotten all about this recording. We'd made it not long after I'd gotten the audio recorder. It was just some fake interview I'd done with Kayla, for fun.

"Just wait 'til school starts," Kayla's voice said. I remember the way the light in her eyes had seemed to sort of dance as she'd said it. She was joking, but then, she wasn't joking at the same time. We'd made the recording just after freshman orientation. We'd just moved into our new apartment, our parents had furnished the place and filled up our kitchen cupboards, and all we had to do, now, was wait for our lives to begin. "Everything's going to be different," Kayla's voice said. "Just wait," she said. "Just wait."

And then, one of the urges came on. Maybe it was hearing Kayla's voice so unexpectedly like that; maybe it was the realization that I would find no answers here, either. Whatever brought it on, I suddenly saw myself turning the steering wheel sharply, veering into the other lane and colliding, head on, with oncoming traffic. I pulled off into the parking lot for the community park and sat in my car. I listened to the rest of the recording. Kayla's voice, hopeful, excited, talking about the movies she was going to make, the campus film club she planned to join. It was a different Kayla—one I had completely forgotten about—than the one who had slit her wrists. When had she changed, and how had I not noticed?

When the recording ended, I climbed out of the car and walked to a bench in the small park. I wanted to listen to the recording again, but I knew it would do no good. Kayla was gone. I held the recorder in my lap and stared at the playground:

the monkey bars, the sandbox, the swings, swaying gently in the breeze. There were two little girls, maybe three or four, climbing up and down the slide from the wrong end. The girls' mothers sat on separate benches, each alternating between tapping away on her phone and glancing up at the girls to call things like, "Corrine, don't put that in your mouth," and, "Megan, play nice." But the girls seemed to be playing nice enough. I watched as one girl, whose hair was long and curly, climbed up the slide while the other, her short, brown hair pulled taut into pigtails, sat at the top of the slide and held out her hands. When the curly-headed girl reached the top, the brunette pushed her back down the slide and then slid down after her. Both girls giggled as they started climbing back up the slide.

Without really understanding why, I started to giggle too. It felt maniacal and weird, but I couldn't help myself. It just felt so funny, all of it: the recording of Kayla, taped over with the Brent interview; the likelihood that I was about to flunk out of school. I was laughing so hard I started to hiccup, and one of the girls' mothers looked over at me. Her blue-grey eyes were sunken and kind of sad, half-moons carved into the skin beneath them. There seemed a kind of wisdom behind those eyes, although she appeared to be mid-twenties, at the oldest. She didn't say anything, and I didn't either. When I regained control of myself, I restarted the recorder at the beginning and pressed the red button. Then I held it up to the sky like a lightning rod until I heard the click of the recorder reaching the end of its capacity. On the drive home later, I listened to what I had left: fifty-four minutes of birds chirping, wind cascading over the microphone, the faraway laughter of two little girls.

THE STRAIGHT AND NARROW

My mom's voice sounds tinny through my dorm phone. Must be the connection. She says, "This is not an easy thing to say," but her words seem to flow comfortably enough. Her voice doesn't sound like she's been crying. Doesn't sound strained or forced, distressed. It's just my mom, her usual flat tone, telling me my dad is gone forever.

I don't say anything, and, I think to fill the silence, she adds, "I just woke up and he isn't breathing. Your father's dead."

Father. I'm trying to put meaning to the word. Why is she calling him by this formal term that calls up images of God, catholic priests?

Matt shifts his position, pulls the blanket a little higher over his bare chest and lets out an unconscious moan. I'm not surprised the phone didn't wake him. I wish I could be such a deep sleeper, so the phone wouldn't have woken me up and I wouldn't be forced to figure out what to say now. "Okay," I say, and it's a stupid thing, an inappropriate thing to say, but it comes out anyway.

One second I was asleep, having the nightmare, the same one I've had since I was a kid. The one about my dad and the funeral pickets. Then suddenly the phone was ringing and I was awake, shivering. Matt had rolled the blanket around himself in his sleep like he always does.

My mom doesn't say anything, and I know I'm supposed to say something more meaningful than "okay." There's some exact way you're supposed to be in this situation, but nothing like this has ever happened to me, and I'm not sure I'm fully awake yet. Maybe I'm not awake at all. Maybe this is a new addition to the dream.

But there's nothing dreamlike about this moment. The clock reads 4:07; you can't see things like that in a dream. And it seems fitting, for some reason, that my dad should be dead. Isn't that the way it works? You have a big fight and before you reconcile, before you even decide if you want to, he's gone. And my mom is waiting for me to say something better than "okay."

"I mean," I say, clear my throat. Buy a few more seconds. "I mean, are you serious?"

She sighs. "I need you to come home right away."

Matt rolls onto his back. I stand up, move over to sit at my desk. As if he instinctively senses my absence, he stretches his slender legs out across my side of the bed, his head still resting on his pillow. His entire body remains rolled up inside the blanket, and he looks like he's inside a cocoon, in the process of metamorphosis. I feel like something is changing inside me too, something I can't control, and all I really want right now is to stop it. Stop my mom from saying any more, stop my dad from being dead, and stop myself from not knowing how to be.

"Is Lillian coming?" I ask.

"I haven't talked to her yet. I'm sure she'll get here as soon as she can."

I don't want to get there first. I don't want to be there just me and my mom. "I have a test tomorrow," I say, and it isn't exactly a lie. I do have a test in Anatomy, but I have something like fifty extra credit points in that class. I'm pretty much guaranteed an A no matter what. I can easily miss this one tiny test, just a quiz, really, and at any rate, Professor Willis would let me retake it.

"Timothy." My mom's voice is calm, but still I know this is a reprimand.

"I'm sorry, Mom," I say quickly. "When is the funeral?"

"I just woke up, Timothy. I just found him dead. You think I've already set a date for the funeral?"

"I just mean, can't I come down tomorrow after the test?" She doesn't say anything for a second, so I add, "My grades have to stay up if I want to keep my scholarship."

"I need you here." There is a finality to her voice. She's daring me to argue.

"Okay," I say. "I'll be there as soon as I can."

"I checked into it. The next departure's 6:25. That gives you some time to pack. You'll arrive at 9:05."

It's a weird feeling, realizing that she checked the bus schedule before she called. It's a logical move, but it doesn't seem like you'd be thinking so logically when you wake up and find your husband of twenty-four years lying cold beside you. It doesn't seem like the first thing on your mind would be arrival and departure times, how much time your son will have to pack.

"Okay," I say for the third time this morning. There is another pause, an aggressive sort of silence. "Mom?"

"I'm sorry," she says, and I don't know what she's sorry about, that my dad is dead or something else. "Travel safe."

"See you soon."

I hang up and stare at Matt for a second. I want to climb back in bed beside him, curl up under the blanket and nuzzle my nose into his neck, breathe in his musk. Forget about everything else. But I can't. I can't wake him yet, either. I'll have to soon. Need him to give me a ride to the bus station. But as soon as he wakes up, I'll have to say it out loud—my dad is dead— and I don't know why, but I can't do it yet.

I go to my closet and pull out my duffel bag. It won't take me long to pack. My closet at home is still full of clothes that I never wear anymore, and I can just wear those, though I know it will feel strange, like stepping back in time. I used to always wear short sleeved, button-down shirts in a single color or a subdued plaid. I used to wear khaki pants with pleats. I don't remember ever making the conscious decision to diversify my closet, as Matt calls it. It was a gradual thing, a t-shirt here, a pair of jeans there. Suspenders. A pinstriped hat with a brim that Matt bought for me, which I know my mom would think I wear to hide my much too long, now, hair.

I can't wear these clothes at home. I would try to get a haircut too, but there's no time for that. My mom won't like it because she won't understand it. I've been planning on cutting my light brown curls, which have formed themselves into ringlets these past few months, before my next visit home. Spring break, I've been assuming. The last time I was home, for Christmas, my mom kept touching my hair and tsking. It was already getting long, and it kept poking into my eyes. Now it's down to my ears, and I feel a twinge of guilt that my mom will have to deal with this on top of everything else.

When I was a kid, she used to tell me, "God's always with you," as she would part my hair down the middle and spit shine it, forcing it flat against my skull. "When you're in the presence of the King, you show a little respect."

This kind of thing is important to my mom: keeping yourself up, having the right appearance. Even though most people would say she's let herself go. She's gained weight exponentially over the past ten years. Even so, she spends hours every morning forcing her frizzy blond curls into submission and painting over her freckles with foundation, making herself right.

But Matt likes them, my ringlets, likes to plunge his fingers into them and twirl them around into even tighter curls. Despite the fact that I've had it in the back of my mind that I would cut my hair before my next visit home, the idea of actually doing it feels painful and wrong.

Still, I have to do something about my hair, so I go to my tiny sink, just a curved slab of porcelain protruding from the wall by the door beneath a scratched and cloudy stainless-steel faucet, and wet my hair down. I slick back the brown spirals with a comb and pull them as best I can into a tight ponytail. I secure it in place with a rubber band and turn to inspect my handiwork in the mirror. The hair in the front doesn't reach back to the rubber band, but it's wet and flattened to my head, at least. The ponytail is short, a tiny tuft of hair that barely even extends beyond the rubber band. It looks ridiculous, but it'll have to do. My mom won't like this either, but it will at least show that I'm trying.

I splash cold water on my face, and as I look back up at the mirror, I can't help but notice how slim my face looks. Last time my mom wanted to know didn't they feed me out here at school. This time she'll probably assume I'm anorexic. I was never overweight, but I like the way I look better this way. Secretly, I think Matt likes it too, although he would never admit that I wasn't perfect to begin with.

I throw on a plain black t-shirt and a pair of dark blue jeans and toss some things into my duffel bag: some neurology books in case I feel like studying, my toothbrush and deodorant, a few shirts and a pair of pants that I probably won't wear.

And then I wake up Matt.

I have to shake him twice before he actually opens his eyes. They're misty and half aware, and his voice is groggy when he smiles up at me and says, "Hmm?"

"Matt." But I have to stop because my voice sounds shaky.

Matt yawns, his defined jaw dropping and then rising again, and then he lifts his hands to my hair and pulls some of it free from its position plastered against my skull. He twists his willowy fingers around a ringlet then moves the curl to rest just near my eyes. "There," he says. "Brings out the blue in your eyes." He reaches back to loosen more of my wet hair and says, "Did you just take a shower?"

I take his hands, kiss them one at a time, and then place them on the blanket and proceed to press my hair back against my head. "No," I say.

He sits halfway up on his elbows, then lifts his right hand up to his own curls, much shorter than mine but tighter and thicker, a brown so deep it's almost black. "What's wrong?" His voice sounds crisp now.

"My dad's dead," I say, and it's funny that my voice sounds clear again. Emotionless. The way my mom's voice sounded a moment ago when she gave the same news to me.

"Shit." It's a response like "okay." It's that not knowing how to react reaction.

"I have to go home. Can you give me a ride to the bus station?"

Without hesitation, he says, "Of course."

Matt gets ready quickly, and by the time we get down to his truck, his eyes are lucid and alert. I climb inside and set my duffel bag at my feet, fiddle around with the seatbelt just to have something to do. Matt puts the truck in gear without saying anything. I'm relieved because I'm not sure, really, if there's anything to say.

I can tell by the way he drums his fingers against the steering wheel, the way he stares straight ahead, that he feels uncomfortable about it all. He doesn't like my dad. He's met my dad only the one time, two weeks ago, but he doesn't like him. The truth is, he has every reason not to, but he probably feels weird about it right now. It was only just last night that I was complaining to Matt about my dad and how he doesn't want me to go into neurology. Matt had sort of gone off on a rant about it all, about the neurology debate and my dad's volunteer work at the homosexuality rehabilitation center back home, the committee my dad formed at my church to picket funerals. Last night Matt said some things that this morning, in light of my dad's death, he might wish he could take back.

I see a falling star shoot from one side of the night sky to the other, carrying behind it a stream of incandescent light. It's supposed to be good luck, seeing a shooting star. You're supposed to make a wish. I stare at the vacant spot in the sky that the star exploded across only seconds ago. It doesn't seem to me like something falling out of the sky can be good.

I turn to Matt, say, "I'm not sure how long I'll be gone," because I want him to know that I haven't forgotten him. That I'm taking his feelings into consideration.

He keeps his eyes on the road and nods. "I'm so sorry, Timmy B."

I say it, too. "I'm sorry." Another inappropriate thing to say.

His eyes dart over to me.

"I'm going to miss you," I say.

"I'm going to miss you, too. You need to be with your family."

"Wish you could be there with me."

"Me too," he says, and his jaw tenses, a quick flex.

Matt and I make the rest of the drive in silence, and when we pull into the bus station parking lot, he drives up to the curb at the entrance instead of into the parking area to find a spot. "Is it okay if I just drop you?" he asks. "This parking lot's a bitch."

"Yeah," I just sit there for a moment, waiting. For a kiss. A hug. Something to take with me on the bus.

"I'm sorry about your dad, Timmy B." His jaw flexes again.

"I know," I say, and then, "I love you."

His brown eyes go soft, and he looks like he's going to cry, but he doesn't. "I love you too," he says and kisses me. A brief kiss, not as deep and reaching as I want, but his soft lips, slightly parted, press against mine for a second, and it's enough for now.

I climb out of the truck, reach my head back in before closing the door and say, "I'll call."

He nods, and I close the door without either of us saying goodbye.

He doesn't wait for me to walk inside to pull away from the curb. I turn to walk toward the doorway, not wanting to stand there and watch him drive away. I had assumed that Matt would come inside and wait with me, but it's just as well. After what happened with my dad the other day, nothing feels quite right between Matt and me, and I guess I'd rather be alone than have this awkwardness sitting like a barrier between us.

I buy my ticket and sit down to wait. The air in the bus station feels thick. I'm not sure whether I'll be able to breathe it for long. It isn't like air at all, really. It's heavy, like water, and warm. It smells like body odor and perfume, like the part you try to hide and the thing you hide it with.

I pull out one of the neurology books I packed, a collection of essays about recent neuroscience studies and their implications. This book is too advanced for a freshman who isn't even allowed yet to take anything but core courses. Prerequisites. I'm halfway through an essay on recent studies about personal will and the brain, but as I try to pick up where I left off before, my mind bounces from thought to thought, and I can't really understand the words in front of me. I read the same sentence four times before I give up. Something about the existence of the soul, whether there can even be such a thing when we already know that most of our decisions stem from subconscious activity going on in the brain. But I can't concentrate on it right now because I keep wondering whether or not my dad has a soul that will live on now though his body is gone. And I wonder whether Matt has one. Whether I do.

I hear the tap tap tapping of a cane feeling its way along the linoleum walkway. Just as my mind begins to tune the sound out, the bench I'm sitting on is jostled by a blind man whose cane has led him astray. He's young, probably early twenties. I don't think I've ever seen someone so young with a cane. The skin on his face is smooth and his features well-defined, sharp, and I think how sad it is that a man should be so handsome and never be able to see his own face.

He turns slightly, repositions himself on the walkway, and holds his cane out so far in front of him that his entire body tilts haphazardly toward the ground. His center of gravity seems to defy physics, extends well beyond where it should be. He looks as though he's in mid fall, caught somewhere between the safety of standing and the finality of the floor. He gently prods the ground with his cane before taking another step.

The thin curtains of skin over his eyes move as the eyes beneath them roll around in place. It looks creepy, like a horror movie where the hero thinks the bad guy's dead but the viewer knows better.

Tap tap tap. Tap tap tap. Tap tap thunk. Tap tap thunk thunk. The blind man's cane prods the carpeting on my side of the walkway. He apparently recognizes the sound, or perhaps the soft give of the carpet, and turns around. But in his fervor to get back on the linoleum, he overcompensates and heads straight for the carpeting on the other side of the walkway.

Tap tap tap. Tap tap tap. Tap tap thunk. Tap thunk thunk. The man stops. Frowning, he turns around once more, but to a lesser degree, and continues his trek along the walkway. This time he's able to stay pretty straight on the linoleum with only an occasional brush against the carpet on the other side, but he's facing the opposite direction from where he had originally been heading. He'll eventually reach his destination, but he's going to have to walk a straight line around the world, first.

Watching the man go by for the second time, I wonder if I should step in and ask him which way he intends to go, point him in the right direction. But I'm not sure if it would come across helpful, as intended, or condescending, as though I'm suggesting the man can't find his way on his own.

I don't want to offend a complete stranger. Plus, the blind man is already well on his way in the wrong direction. At this point, any offer to help would be so belated it would come across patronizing. He's bound to get wherever he's headed sooner or later. I sit and listen as the tapping fades into imperceptibility.

I look back down at my book. The words just sort of merge together on the page. They dance and flow, and I can't distinguish any one word from the next. I know it's probably supposed to be that way. I'm not supposed to be reading right now or thinking about anything but the grief that I don't even feel yet.

I should be thinking about my dad, about the fight we had the last time we saw each other or wondering if his death had anything to do with stress, anything to do with me. But I don't want to think about that. The angry words. My dad's red face. My dad grasping at Matt's bare shoulder, squeezing his tan skin, fingernails digging in. Matt's taut skin turning white, tearing a little. And later—after Matt left and after I drove my dad to the hospital and after they bandaged my dad's nose—my dad not wanting to talk to me. Not even wanting to look at me. My dad driving off without saying goodbye. And I'm not even thinking about Matt, how he didn't want to wait to see me off. Instead, as I sit and wait for the bus that will take me home, I can't stop thinking about my hair, how long it's gotten and how my mom isn't going to like it. That and the blind man who is headed in the wrong direction.

Lillian is already there when I arrive. I'm surprised because she and my dad never really got along; I'd half expected her not to come at all. But I'm relieved, all the same. She and my mom are playing cribbage, of all things, and after some hugs and a "look at you," a disapproving twist of a ringlet from my mom, I'm able to disappear upstairs on the pretense of needing a shower. The wall along the staircase is peppered with pictures of me from different stages in my childhood. There's one with me and Lillian sitting in front of the Christmas tree, but all the other pictures are just me posing alone. When I became an official member of the church, when I caught my first fish. At the top of the stairs is the most recent one: when I graduated from the Academy.

My parents' door is open, and I can't help but think how my dad was in there, dead, just hours ago. I pick up the pace to get to my room—the guest room. That's what it is now. The door is closed, and when I place my hand on the knob, I have the dizzying feeling like the world is pitching forward and I'm staying still. I have to steady myself against the door for a second before I can push it open. The bed is covered with an unfamiliar brown and red patchwork quilt. It's one of those quilts you buy in a plastic bag at a department store, the kind that's created to look homemade but isn't. It's made in a factory somewhere alongside thousands of other quilts that look exactly like it.

I sit on the bed. Everything in the room except the new quilt is the same as I left it last fall. The nightstand is here, and sitting on it are the same lamp and alarm clock I used the entire time I was at the Academy. The framed picture of my dad and me fishing when I was ten is here. All the things that I left behind, all the things I didn't think worth taking. But now, next to the picture, there is a little dish of scented oil, and the entire room smells like lavender.

I walk down the stairs with my hair still wet. My fresh slacks and button-up shirt are stiff and uncomfortable from having hung unworn for so long. In the living room, both Lillian and my mom are mesmerized by something on the TV. Lillian sits on the couch, leaning forward, her elbows pressing into her thighs, and my mom stands, her head cocked.

On the TV, a tanned newswoman with big, wig-like hair stands on the side of the road in front of Resurrection Bridge; a group of police officers mill around in the background. "The body has been positively identified as fourteen-year-old Travis Townsend," she says in that phony, newscaster way, emphasizing the wrong syllables and sounding emotionless, robotic. Her image is replaced by what appears to be a school photograph of a curly-haired, blue-eyed boy. His cheeks are rosy and his lips chapped and red. So young and innocent looking, this boy, who is being described now as "the body."

Lillian leans even further forward. "He looks just like Timothy," she says. "Don't you think? Don't you guys think?"

My mom doesn't say anything, and I just sort of shrug, but he *does* look like me, a younger, more self-assured version. He stares at the camera with eyes bright and unashamed, and his smile is pure.

The woman comes back on the screen. "I'm here with Officer Pete Johnston." The camera pulls back to reveal a policeman standing beside the newswoman. "Thank you for talking to me, Officer."

"It's fine," he says stiffly, looking into the camera.

"Officer Johnston, does the police department have any idea yet what happened?"

"It's clear that the death was not an accident," he says. "The body is covered in bruises and lacerations."

"No chance that this may have been a suicide?"

Officer Johnston shakes his head. "There's indication of struggle, and the sorts of bruises the body has sustained couldn't have been made from him jumping from the bridge. This is clearly a homicide."

"Does the police department have any idea who might have done such a thing?"

"I can't release any information on that right now," Johnston says.

"No leads?"

"I can't release any such information."

"Anything you'd like to say to the victim's family?"

Officer Johnston hesitates, shifts from one foot to the other, then says, "Rest assured that we will find the perpetrator. Anyone with any information should contact us."

"Alright, thank you." Before Officer Johnston can respond, the camera zooms in on the newswoman again. "We'll keep you posted as the story unfolds."

The screen changes to a newsroom with a model-like man sitting behind the desk. "Thanks so much, JoAnn. Do the police have any idea how long the body's been hidden there?"

The screen divides to show JoAnn again, and there is a pause as she presses the palm of her hand up to her ear. Finally, she says, "It's too early to know for sure, Tom, but the body has clearly been here for several days. Travis Townsend was reported missing about a week ago."

Tom shakes his head. "Absolutely tragic."

"It certainly is, Tom. My sources say that there's reason to believe this may have been a hate crime. The boy was a homosexual."

"Shit," Lillian says.

My mom, who I would have expected to reprimand her, stares at the screen, chews her lip, doesn't say anything at all.

After my mom goes to bed and Lillian disappears into her room, I head downstairs to the den and jump on Snapchat to see if Matt's online. He isn't, but I'm not sleepy, so I refresh my Insta feed five times and like most everybody I know from school's most recent tweet. Matt's simply reads, "Missing Timmy B." I click the Comment button but just stare at the blinking cursor for a second before clicking away again. My most recent tweet reads, "Seriously intoxicated right now by the smell of Matt's homemade lasagna." I feel embarrassed for posting something so banal just days before my father died, and I click delete.

On an impulse, though I don't really want to think any more about it, I find myself opening a fresh Chrome tab, typing Travis Townsend's name into the search box. There are 613,498 results, only the first handful of which have anything to do with the person I'm looking for, and even fewer say anything about the murder. I open the first link, an article from today's *Recorder*, and scan through the text. I'm not sure what I'm hoping to find, but the information is the same as what the lady said on TV: fourteen-year-old boy, open homosexual, foul play suspected. The photo of Travis Townsend in the paper is the same as the one they showed on TV, and it's true: the boy looks like a younger version of me. Looked.

I go back to the search results and open another article, this one from the public high school's newspaper, a special edition. It contains all the same information, with the addendum that the victim was not a student at Harsville High but may have been friends with some of the H.H.S. students. Counseling will be available for those students who are personally affected by the loss, and it goes on.

It's strange that he wasn't an H.H.S. student. The only other high school in town is the Academy, and it seems unlikely that an open homosexual would go there, although maybe that would explain the murder. Thinking back to my time at the Academy, it's possible that a group of students—maybe even a teacher—might do something like that in the name of purging sin. At the Academy they refer to homosexuals as "the devil's children," a title culled from a film they made us watch every year in the auditorium. In the movie, the devil sends a group of his minions into the world to corrupt the masses. They go around encouraging homosexual experimentation among boys and men—there are no female homosexuals in the film, probably because everybody knew that, even if you put a negative spin on it, most of the teenaged boys in the audience would get aroused at the thought of lesbian activities. At the end of the movie, God creates AIDS to punish the devil's children, and after turning it off, the principle would give the same speech every year, about what we should have learned from the movie.

If people at the Academy really believed that God created AIDS to punish the homosexuals of the world, it didn't seem unthinkable that they might beat to death a homosexual boy enrolled at their school. I do a search for Travis Townsend and the Harsville Academy, but it brings up the same results as when I searched for Travis's name alone.

I retype "Travis Townsend" into the search bar and sit for a second, deciding what else to check the name against. I type in "and," then lean back and gaze around the room, searching for inspiration. The den is a tiny square room with just the computer desk and two rolling chairs, all of which my dad found for cheap at a garage sale. The only real splash of personality in the room is created by the foot long bulletin board hanging on the wall behind the computer. Secured to the board by push pins are photographs of the family and people from the church. A photo of Pastor Nathan and my dad shaking hands. A photo of my dad leaning against the church van, an upside down picket sign propped against his leg. A candid shot of my dad and the other members of his church committee standing outside a funeral home.

The people in this photo—though they all look nice enough, smiling and laughing and energetically talking—would, moments later, have pulled their picket signs out of the back of the church van and begun thrusting them in the faces of the mourners leaving the wake. The photo must be an old one; I can tell not only because my dad's skin seems smoother, his hair denser, his body weight a good fifty pounds lighter, but because the committee stopped picketing at funeral homes and churches several years ago; the cops told them they had to. Private property. They could only go to cemeteries, and even then, they had to keep a comfortable distance between themselves and the mourners. "Freedom of speech only gets you so far," my dad told me once, shaking his head. "Forget the fact that we're trying to save people's souls."

I don't know whether the people on my dad's committee believe that AIDS was created to punish homosexuals, but they would surely approve of the title "devil's children." Still, I know these people. It's hard for me to imagine them—Bob Morgan, who owns the donut shop downtown and who always brought me free day-old donuts when he'd come by the house, or Nancy Keenan, who knits during church and donates about a sweater a week to the church clothing drive—beating a fourteen-year-old boy to death, devil's child or not. Plus, I don't see how any of them would have known Travis Townsend. The only member of the committee, to my knowledge, who might ever come into contact with an out homosexual is my dad, at the rehab.

I turn back to the computer and type in "Christian Soldier's Homosexuality Rehabilitation Center" and hit enter. Bingo. The very first result is a press release, put out by the C.S.H.R.C. director today, lamenting the loss of their patient, Travis Townsend, who disappeared from the center a week ago. "We have no reason to assume that Travis's murder was in any way linked to his treatment at the center," the press release reads, "as all signs point to the boy's disappearance as a voluntary, self-discharge." So that's it. Travis wasn't from Harsville at all; his parents had probably committed him to the center against his will, and he had run away.

So then, I wonder if my dad knew him. I wonder if my dad marveled at the resemblance between his very own son, born of his own flesh, and this openly homosexual boy. I picture my dad seeing Travis for the first time, shaking his head and thinking how unfortunate it is that his son and this boy would look so much alike. This boy who was so young and had already veered so far from the path of righteousness. And what if my dad had run into Travis just after his last visit with me? Did the resemblance, maybe, take on a new meaning?

A throat clears behind me, and I jump, reflexively laying my phone screen down on my lap. I spin around to find Lillian looking over my shoulder. "Not tired?"

I shake my head.

"Me either." She sits on the other rolling chair and folds her arms. "You think Mom is sleeping in her bed?"

"Why wouldn't she?"

"Doesn't it seem kind of creepy?"

"She might be sleeping on the floor," I say, but I know it probably isn't true. "But it's not like the bed is haunted."

"I know," she says. "Still. I wouldn't sleep in a bed that had a dead body in it. What're you up to?"

I lift up my phone, screen still aimed down, and shrug.

"I have an idea," she says, rolling her chair over to the dusty desktop computer. She opens a browser window and types our dad's name into the search field. The search brings up 917,985 results.

"What idea?"

"I think we should see what kind of legacy Dad left behind." She scrolls through the first ten results, all of which are articles from the Recorder about funeral pickets led by my dad: "At the head of the angry procession was James Bannister . . ." "Leading the picketers was anti-homosexual activist James Bannister . . ." "James Bannister, the leader of the mob, declined to comment on the events."

I sigh. "What did you expect to find?"

"I don't know," Lillian says, clicking on an article, skimming it, then clicking back and skimming through another. Then she turns to face me. "I guess I expected to find this. I was just curious."

"This is what he's leaving behind."

She nods. "That this is the impact he's made on the world."

I want to argue. Feel like I should point out that there was more to my dad than just the funeral pickets, or that a life cannot so easily be summarized by the top ten Google search results. But I can't stop thinking about Travis Townsend, about the fact that my dad could have known him.

"I thought maybe there would be something on here about his police file," Lillian says, turning back to the computer, then clicking the arrow to see the next set of results.

"I doubt that kind of thing is online," I say. "Seems like an invasion of privacy."

"True," she says. "I didn't know if maybe the Recorder might have reported on it or something."

"What difference does it make?"

She shrugs. "Just think it's interesting. Don't you?"

"Why?"

"Because this is all that's left of him now. Or this is what's left that is still publicly available. And as time ticks on and the people who knew him think about him less and less, this will really become all there is that remains of James Bannister. Makes you think."

"As in, we are nothing more or less than our actions?"

"Exactly," she says, and clicks to see the next page, and then the next page of results. "Hey, what did that guy's bumper sticker say? The guy Dad beat up?"

"He didn't beat him up," I say. "It said 'Straight but not narrow.'"

She types "and straight but not narrow" next to my dad's name in the search field, then hits enter. Nothing new comes up. "You don't remember the date Dad was arrested, do you?"

I shake my head.

She searches for the Harsville Recorder Police Blotter and scans through the archives. "That would have been when you were, what, fourteen?"

"Twelve," I say. "Or so."

She clicks on the year 2016, then quickly skims through the month of January.

"This is a waste of time," I say. "And pointless."

"A-ha!" she says, and points to an entry from February 22nd, 2016.

"A man was charged with a hate crime today, police say. The victim reported being followed to the parking lot outside the Barotta Pines apartment complex. The assailant proceeded to berate the victim for displaying a bumper sticker promoting homosexual rights. The assailant then assaulted the victim and is being held overnight in the Dreydon County Jail."

"So? It doesn't even have his name. This isn't part of his legacy, by your own definition."

"Okay." She laughs. "I'll give you that."

"And he didn't stay in jail overnight," I add. "Mom paid his bail. They let him out like an hour after it happened."

"Okay. Okay." She holds her palms out. "But that's not really the point, is it? The point is that he was charged with a hate crime. He went to jail. And if we're really trying to tally up who Dad was, we should probably take that into consideration."

"Nobody asked you to tally up who dad really was." I stand.

"Isn't that what you do when someone dies?"

"I don't know," I say. "I've never known anyone who died. And I've definitely never had someone close to me die, let alone my own dad."

"Don't get defensive," she says. "I'm just saying."

I force a yawn and stretch. "I'm going to bed."

Lillian reaches out her hand and touches my forearm. "Hey, don't be mad, okay? I'm only half serious."

"I know."

"It's just something to think about," she says.

I nod and then head up the stairs. I pause outside my mom's bedroom but conquer the urge to peek inside and see whether she is sleeping on the bed. Instead, I head to my own bedroom, lie down on my bed and stare up at the ceiling, and wonder what I would find if I googled my own name, whether it would tell me something about who I really am.

The parking lot at the C.S.H.R.C. is swarming with people picketing the center's existence. I guess it's not surprising that a place like this would have opponents, but I'm sure they're here today because of Travis Townsend. I sit in the driver's seat of my dad's car for a moment, the engine running. Try to will myself to turn the ignition off and walk inside. I need to do this, to go in and talk to the people my dad volunteered beside, but I feel embarrassed that I've never stopped by before, and the truth is I'm afraid that somebody will guess the reason why. I turn off the engine but instead of climbing out of the car, I pull my cell phone out of my pocket and call Matt.

I listen to the air crackle as my line finds Matt's, then listen to it ring and then ring and ring, but I turn it off when Matt's voice comes on because all it will do is ask me to leave a message, and I don't know where to begin. I drop my phone back in my pocket and climb out of the car.

With an imposing five floors, the C.S.H.R.C. is the tallest building in Harsville, and it casts a shadow around everything that ventures near it. It's brown and plain and completely unremarkable, except that the words Christian Soldiers' Homosexuality Rehabilitation Center hang in deep red letters above the entrance. People come from all around to seek aid at the C.S.H.R.C. There are two separated sects of patients: minors, whose parents checked them in and, in my understanding, most of whom are there against their will, and adults, mostly middle-aged men, according to my dad, who lived for a long time with their "sin" before finally admitting that they need help.

I keep my eyes trained on the asphalt as I make my way past the picketers. They're marching around in chaotic lines and thrusting signs in the air, but they aren't yelling the way my dad and everyone used to yell at the funeral pickets. These people don't know how to hold their signs at the right angle, so the most people will be able to see them. They don't know that you have to make noise if you want to get noticed.

Just before the entrance, someone takes hold of my shoulder, but it isn't a violent gesture. It's a gentle squeeze. "There's nothing wrong with you, son," a man's voice says into my ear. I don't look up as I hurry through the front doors.

Once I step into the waiting room, I squint to get accustomed to the dim lighting. The room is decked out just like the waiting room at a doctor's office—round backed chairs with minimal cushions and knee-height, circular tables. Aligned in carefully thought-out patterns on top of the tables are magazines, which are all Christian themed. *God's Children. Trinity. The Way and the Light.*

There are two policemen up at the front desk, and I hesitate, not sure if it's okay for me to approach. I decide to take a seat while I wait my turn, and I grab a magazine from the nearby table so that I can better pretend that I'm not eavesdropping. I pull it open to a full-page advertisement for WWJD jewelry. The ad displays a group of teenaged kids clustering around a girl with thick glasses and braces who is raising her arm to show off a glittery bracelet dangling from her wrist. "Impress God AND your friends!"

"You don't have a record of who the last person to see Travis was?" one of the cops says to the lady behind the desk.

The lady's thick glasses, big and round, magnify her eyes so much that I can't tell whether she's looking the cop in the eyes as she answers. "I'm sorry, but we don't. As you can imagine, we had no way of knowing that something like this might happen to the boy."

The other cop leans in toward her. "We'll need to look at whatever records you *do* have regarding Travis Townsend."

"All of our records are confidential. As I'm sure you're aware, it's the law."

"And as I'm sure *you're* aware, a fourteen-year-old boy has been beaten to death and thrown off a bridge," one of the cops says. "He was committed into *your* facility's care. Are you going to aid the investigation willingly or should we go back to the office and get a warrant?"

The woman frowns. "I think you should go back and get a warrant." She plasters on a phony smile. "That *is* proper procedure, isn't it?"

The cops look at each other, and then one of them knocks on the top of the desk. "We'll be back."

I pull a small notepad and a pen out of my pocket as I approach the front desk. The secretary has begun to type frantically. She makes one last, bold keystroke before acknowledging me. She looks up and tilts her head down to look over the top of her glasses. "Can I help you, young man?"

"I'm, uh." My voice cracks. I clear my throat. "I'm James Bannister's son."

"We don't allow visitors," she says and then pauses. "Oh. Oh, James. Oh."

"Yeah."

She shakes her head. "I was so sorry to hear about your dad. And look how young you are. What a tragedy."

The locker room is musty and dark, the kind of place where things can hide forever. Each locker is about six feet tall. They almost look like a row of metal coffins. The woman with the glasses introduces me to a stocky man named Norm, who takes me to my dad's locker and bangs on the top. The door pops open.

Norm steps aside. "I'll grab you a box." He vanishes into a back room.

I look into the cluttered locker. Photographs pasted to the inside of the door, trinkets piled up on each shelf. I look at the photos. At the top is my graduation photo from the Academy: me in my cap and gown. My dad told my mom that this photo session was a waste of money, that my diploma was proof enough that I had made it, but she insisted. And now, here is the photo taped inside the door of his locker, above all the other photos. I peel the photo off the metal. Norm coughs behind me, and I twirl around. He hands me a large cardboard box. I bend down to place it on the floor, where I can fill it more easily with the contents of my dad's locker.

"Might find it's mostly junk," he says. "But go ahead and empty it out. Anything you don't want you may as well toss."

I pull a picture of my dad and Pastor Nathan from the inside of the door and drop it into the box. I look at all the seemingly random litter on the bottom shelf. A cross keychain. A tiny stuffed monkey in a tight-fitting purple t-shirt. A small stack of C.S.H.R.C. pamphlets. A slightly crumpled Post-It that has, "Love is patient, love is kind," scrawled in unrecognizable handwriting. I scoop everything on the bottom shelf into the box without picking through any more of it, then run my arm along the second and third shelves of the locker, knocking all of their contents into the box, too. "I guess if it was important to him," I say.

Norm nods. "You might not be ready to go through all that yet. Maybe after a little more time has passed."

I pick up the box. "My mom wants me to say a few words. You know, at the funeral. Anything you can tell me about my dad that might help me paint a full picture of who he was?"

Norm shrugs. "You know, each person has many different versions of themselves. I'll bet the way you are around your mom is completely different than how you are around your buddies at school, or your lady friend, if you've got one."

"Yeah."

"Well, maybe that's just the way it is, you know?"

But he must see on my face that I don't.

"It's just natural," he says. "I think maybe you should just remember your dad however you knew him. Whatever version of him he showed to you."

"And the rest doesn't matter?"

"Well, it shouldn't matter to you."

I look down at the overfilled box. It hardly weighs a thing. "Thanks," I say, and, "Uh, hey, Norm?"

"Yes, son?"

"Um, do you know anything about that Travis Townsend kid?"

He doesn't say anything for a second. "What sort of information were you looking for?" he finally says, but his voice is slow and cautious.

"Oh, nothing specific. I just heard about him on the news, and I know that he was a patient here. So."

"Yes," Norm says. "His parents enrolled him in the program."

"Involuntarily?"

"He disappeared from here about a week ago, and we have every reason to assume that he just ran away. As to what happened to him after, I can't say. Must have gotten involved with some bad people out on the street."

I nod. "Um, do you know if my dad knew him?"

He stares into my eyes. "Your father was not permitted direct contact with any of the patients."

I fight the urge to look down.

Norm glances away. "I'm sure he'd seen him, yes. But no, son, your father didn't *know* him."

I look into the box. "My dad," I say, but stop. I'm trying to put together the words. Trying to figure out how to articulate the thoughts that are racing through my mind right now. "Is there any chance that someone from here might have," but I don't finish.

Norm raises one eyebrow at me and cocks his head. He knows exactly where I'm going with this, but he's going to make me say it.

"The police out there," I tilt my head toward the door. "They seemed to think the center's records might help them figure out who did it."

Norm presses his lips together. "Is there a question you wanted to ask?"

I sigh. "Never mind. It was a stupid question, anyway."

"Well," he says, his face a mask of faux friendliness, "let me know if there's anything else I can help you with," which is what people say when they're trying to get rid of you. He holds out his hand to shake mine. I wrestle with the box, trying to maneuver around it, but I can't manage. He holds his palm up to me, shaking his head. "It's okay," he says. "Don't worry about it." He pats me on the back.

When I get home from the rehab, the house is quiet. "Hello?" I call, even though it's obvious that nobody is home. I can only hear the grandfather clock ticking, the hum of the heater.

I carry the box of my dad's stuff upstairs to my mom's room and hesitate when I find the door closed. "Mom?" I shift the box onto my knee and knock. "Mom? You in there?" My parents' door is never closed. When we were little, they used to close it only when they were having sex. They called it "Mommy and Daddy time." But I can't even remember the last time I've seen this door closed.

I turn the knob and push the door open, but I stand in the hallway for a second more. I'm only here to drop off my dad's stuff, and I'm not a little kid anymore. Still, I feel like setting foot inside the room is forbidden—why else would my mom have closed the door? I shake the thought off and force myself to make that first step, and then another, until I'm standing beside the bed. I lay the box down on the bedspread and smooth my hands over the place my dad used to sleep.

I step over to the closet, slide the door open slowly to avoid making any sound, though there is nobody around to hear it. I drop to my knees and begin to search for a sign. Proof. A blood-stained shirt, maybe, or a battered paperweight with the C.S.H.R.C. logo printed on it. If this were a movie or a detective story, there would be some sort of incriminating evidence lying around that I could find and I could point to and I could say, "I knew it was true!" But there is nothing. At least, nothing that I can find.

By the time I hear the door creak open downstairs, followed by my mom and Lillian's distant chatter, I have all but torn this room apart looking for clues. I've looked in every drawer, unearthed a mountain of dust bunnies from under the bed, and rummaged through all of the clothes and miscellany in my parents' closet, and I'm exactly where I started.

"Timothy?" my mom calls from the stairwell. "You home?"

"Yeah," I say, but it comes out like a nervous croak. I clear my throat. "Upstairs." I hurry back over to the bed and put my hands on either side of the box.

I hear my mom's footsteps down the hallway, and the creaking of the guestroom door.

"In here," I call. "In your room."

She appears in the doorway and cocks her head. "Oh." She walks inside. "Oh," she says again when her eyes catch the box.

I rattle its contents. "Cleared out Dad's locker at the center."

She walks to the bed and peers inside the box. "Huh." She sits down on the bed. "I hadn't even thought about his locker." She takes the box from me and tilts it to look inside. The junk inside the box shifts. "I don't really know what we're supposed to do with it."

I shrug. "I didn't know if you would want them to throw it away."

"Yeah," she says. "I guess you're not supposed to just throw things like this away." She stands up, and then lifts the box and drops it with a thud onto the floor. "Guess I'll just hang on to it for now." She crouches down and pushes the box under the bed and then slides her palms down the thighs of her pants as though touching the box has made them dirty.

"You can throw it out if you want."

"Seems wrong, doesn't it? Seems like these things should mean something to me."

I nod and don't say anything.

In the waiting area outside of the church offices, the air feels recycled and unbreathable. The large aquarium that's been here forever and ever is here still but it's got three sucker fish thrown into the mix. They cling to the walls of the tank and pull themselves up and down and sideways and backwards, wiping everything in their paths clean.

Other than the sucker fish, things in the waiting area are unchanged. The paintings on the walls—one of Jesus, one of the last supper—and the lavender paint with white trim, which always makes it feel like Easter. That's exactly, Pastor Nathan told me once, what it's supposed to do since Easter is the mark of the rebirth of Christ. It's a reminder of redemption.

It's eerie, this sameness, because I want to believe that the stuffiness in the air is new, but I realize it must not be. It must always have been here. I must be the one who's changed.

I step up to the front desk where the church secretary, Ida, is typing on her computer. She has a gigantic nose, Ida, and a tiny little head. She turns her pale blue eyes up at me and says, "Oh, hi, Timothy."

"Hi, Ida," I say. I lean against the counter, the palms of my hands supporting my weight.

She squints and says, "I'm so sorry about your dad."

"Thanks," I say. "How are you?"

She leans into me conspiratorially. "This whole Travis Townsend thing has got the phones ringing off the hook."

I glance at the phone. I don't hear anything.

She laughs. "I had to set it to voicemail so I could get some work done. There's always so much to do for a funeral." She blushes a bit after she says it, probably worried she shouldn't have said something like that to the son of the deceased.

I nod to let her know it's okay, that I'm starting to learn the same thing. "Why is everybody calling about Travis Townsend?"

She shakes her head. "People *from* the church are calling because they're all worked up that there was actually a murder in Harsville. People who *aren't* from the church are calling because they're convinced it must have been something to do with, well, you know, with your father's committee." She bats the idea away like a fly with her hand. "It's ridiculous."

"Well," I say, "I guess it's understandable," trying hard to keep the fact from showing in my voice that I've been wondering about that, too. "Pastor Nathan around?"

She glances at Pastor Nathan's closed door and shakes her head. "He's doing house calls."

House calls. Like a doctor. It's funny how, now that I've been away for a while, certain things about the church suddenly strike me as absurd. "I just needed to talk to him."

Ida nods.

"I guess I should come back later," I say.

Ida wrinkles her forehead. "I'm not sure when he'll be back today. I could call his cell, but . . ."

I drum my fingers against the counter. "I guess it's not that important. It's just that my mom says Pastor Nathan wanted me to write this eulogy thing."

She nods.

I let my eyes wander the room. "I'm kind of having trouble with it."

"How do you mean?"

I pull my hands off of the counter and see that there are two small wet circles of sweat where my palms were. I rub the circles out with my forearm. "I'm just not sure what to say."

"Well, you just talk about your dad," she says. "Just talk about how you feel."

"I went to the C.S.H.R.C. to get some outside perspective on him. But."

"You don't need to worry about what other people thought about him," she says. "This is about *your* feelings. What he meant to *you*."

There's no way I'll be able to make her see that that's just the problem: that I don't know how I feel about my dad. I nod and say, "Yeah, that makes sense."

"If you need anything," she says, but she says it like it's a complete statement, not the fragment that it is. Like it makes sense on its own.

"Thanks," I say and walk over to the aquarium. The sucker fish are scattered apart, sucking on different parts of the glass. "When did you guys get these sucker fish?"

"Few months ago," Ida says, without looking up. "They're ugly little things, aren't they? But they keep the tank clean."

Even as I pull into the parking lot, park my dad's car, and walk slowly into the main office, I don't really know what I'm doing at the police station. When it first occurred to me to stop by, I was thinking that I would ask for any information they might be able to give me regarding Travis Townsend, but I can't think of a single reason why they would tell me anything, since I'm no relation to Travis and have no connection to the investigation. But even though I vetoed the idea as soon as it came to me, I found myself climbing into the car and driving to the police station anyway.

I've only actually been inside the police station once, when my dad was arrested for the hate crime all those years ago. It's odd being here now because it's my dad that has brought me here once again. I can't say that it looks like I remember it because I don't remember it, not very well, but it looks like a small-town police station should look—a small room and a sweet looking, elderly policewoman sitting at a front desk. She has a cloud of white hair resting on top of her head, and she isn't behind a thick wall of glass or anything like that. She's reading when I step through the front door, but she lays her book face down on her desk as soon as she sees me and smiles. "Hi there. What can I do for you?"

I glance around the room to make sure that we're alone. "Hi." My tongue sticks to the roof of my mouth, and as I peel it back down again, I fiddle with a stack of pamphlets sitting on the edge of her desk: AA information.

Her smile loosens. "Is everything alright, hon?"

I shake my head. "My dad is James Bannister," I say, and watch her face closely, looking for signs of recognition.

She just nods. Her expression remains fixed.

"He, uh, he owned Bannister's Diner?"

"Ah, yes. Okay," she says, but still doesn't seem to know who my dad was.

"He died yesterday," I say.

She tsks. "Oh, I'm so sorry to hear that." She reaches out and pats my hand.

"Thanks."

"That's just terrible." She pauses and stares at me. Finally, she says, "Was there," and hesitates, squints and looks up at the ceiling for a second.

I look around the empty waiting room again. There isn't anybody else there, but I lean into the desk anyway and say in a voice not much above a whisper, "I need to talk to somebody about my dad. I think he might have, think he killed Travis Townsend."

"Just a moment." She stands up and walks swiftly down the hallway into the back.

When she returns, she's followed closely by a man in uniform with a visible gun hanging on a belt on either side of his hip. He walks around the front desk and holds his hand out to me. "Sheriff Angstrom."

I shake his hand. "Timothy Bannister."

"Bannister," he says to himself.

"James Bannister's son," I say. "He died yesterday."

Sheriff Angstrom nods. "Right. James Bannister. I'm familiar. Eunice here says you had something you wanted to talk to me about?"

I nod. "Yes, I think-"

But he holds his palm out to me and shakes his head. "Would you like to come back to my office, son?"

I follow him into his tiny office, which is cramped with tall filing cabinets lining the walls. His desk takes up half the room, and he has to close the door and then drag a chair in front of it so that there is room for me to sit down. I do, and instead of sitting in his cushy looking, high-backed chair on the other side of his desk, he positions himself in a half-seated position leaning against the desk, just in front of me.

"So what can I do for you, Tim?" he asks, and I can tell by the way he leans in close and stares intently into my eyes that he already knows why I'm here. Surely Eunice told him. But he must have to hear me say it or something. Maybe he wants to make sure that Eunice heard me right.

"Well, my dad died yesterday," I say.

"Yes, I'm sorry to hear about that," he says, but his voice is pinched. I can tell he wants me to get on with it. His fists clench and unclench in his lap.

"I just got back into town yesterday morning," I say. "I came down for the funeral."

He nods. "Uh-huh?"

I lean back in the chair and glance around the small office. "And then I heard about Travis Townsend."

He opens his eyes and nods again. Looks at me closely and leans back a bit more.

"I hope this doesn't sound crazy," I say, "but I felt like I should come talk to someone. Because I think my dad may have killed him. Travis."

There is a silence as the sheriff looks me up and down. Finally, he asks me, "Can you walk me through what it is that makes you think that?"

"They said, on the news they said it was a hate crime."

"I know who your father is, Tim," he says, standing. "Was." He walks around to his desk and drops into his comfortable-looking chair. He folds his hands in front of him on the desk. "You should know, though, that we haven't really determined yet whether Travis Townsend's murder was a hate crime. The media kind of took the idea and ran with it. Sensationalizing. But we're not really sure. It's one of many possibilities."

"It's not just because they said it was a hate crime," I say. "My dad, he volunteered at the C.S.H.R.C. Travis Townsend disappeared from there about a week ago."

He leans forward in his chair. "If you'll forgive me, Tim, it doesn't really sound to me like you have any concrete reason to believe it was your dad."

"Well, there's more," I start, but stop myself. If I bring up the striking resemblance between me and Travis Townsend—which he must surely have already noticed himself—and if I tell him about the fight, I'll have to tell him, too, what the fight was about.

"Yes?" he says.

"Never mind."

He stares at me for a second and then leans back again. "I do appreciate you coming by, Tim, and again, I'm very sorry to hear about your father." He stands up. "If you come across any," he waves his hand in the air, and I imagine he is thinking "real evidence" though he doesn't say it, "don't hesitate to be in touch."

I stand up. "Thanks," I say, reaching out to shake his hand again.

He steps around the desk and takes my hand, gives it a firm squeeze and then drops his other hand onto my elbow and leans in, says, "Thanks for coming, Tim." He holds my elbow in his tight grip and seems to be trying to decide whether or not to say something. After a second, he says, "Don't worry yourself about the investigation. We know what we're doing. But I want you to know that I think it says a lot about you that you came in here today."

I nod. "Thanks," I say, and then show myself out.

I wake up from a nightmare that I can only remember in vague flashes, images which don't make any sense as I try to piece them together. I check the time on the clock. 3:24 AM. Today is the day that we will bury my dad. I sit up and wipe sweat from my forehead with my arm and look around the room, letting the grey images come into focus in the dim light. Then I grab my notebook and pen from the bedside table, wrap my blanket around myself and walk downstairs. I walk into the kitchen and flick on the light.

I sit down and drop the notebook on the table in front of me, flip it open to the page where I have several crossed out starts to my eulogy.

~~My dad was the sort of man you could count on to always do the right thing.~~
~~My dad loved his family above all else.~~
~~My dad was the ultimate role model for his children.~~
~~My dad did everything in his power to make the world a better place.~~

It all feels false, and I won't be able to say it when it comes time. But I don't know what I *will* be able to say, don't know what I could say that is both true and appropriate for a funeral. I can't tell them that I've spent the past two days wondering whether my dad murdered a fourteen-year-old kid, and I can't tell them that my dad and I had a huge fight because he didn't approve of my life up at school, or the fact that he alienated his own daughter just because she wasn't Christian.

And I know that there are other things, better things, that I could say about him. I could talk about how close my dad and I were, how he used to take me fishing, or how, even though he didn't want me to go into neurology, he still agreed to pay for my dorm so I could focus on my studies. How he loved me. And I loved him back. So why can't I think of what to say at his funeral?

I tap my pen against the notebook, then pull off the cap and scribble a tornado at the top of the page. Below that I sketch a monster with gleaming, blood dripping fangs. I picture myself standing at the front of the church in a few short hours, half the congregation of the church staring up at me. In my mind, I hold up my notebook, which by then I would have filled with awkward drawings, and say, "This is how I feel about my dad."

I shake my head and throw the pen against the pad. "Come on," I say out loud. "Just write something."

I hear a door creak open upstairs and I freeze, sit in silence for a moment as the carpet in the hallway pops, then the light in the upstairs bathroom clicks on, with the fan that always kicks on with it, and the bathroom door swings closed.

I pick the pen back up and make a big X through the current notebook page, then flip to the next page and position the tip of the pen at the top. I drag the pen down, making an "I," then cross it out. I write "My dad," then cross that out, too, and sigh. I lean back in the chair and toss the pen onto the table.

At first, I can't move. I'm glued to my seat, and my palms and forehead are slick and clammy. But Pastor Nathan has already stepped down from the pulpit, moved to the side and taken his seat near the organist. There is nothing to do but move straight ahead, step up to the pulpit, and say what I have to say.

When I get to the front and turn around and place my hands firmly on the pulpit's smooth wooden surface, I feel jolted by all the staring eyes. For a second, I say nothing and watch a fly dance around the church's vaulted ceiling. I can hear cloth brush against cloth as someone uncrosses and then re-crosses his legs. I hear someone cough, a pew creaking as someone shifts in their seat. I clear my throat into the microphone and the sound, magnified, bounces back at me. "Excuse me," I say and then close my mouth again, watching the people watch me. I straighten my tie and look back up at the fly zigzagging along the stained glass windows.

I feel in my pocket and pull out my notebook, which still holds nothing more than crossed out lines and doodles. The moment is here, my time up, and I never wrote my eulogy. I glance down at the notebook and then back up. "Um, I had some things planned," I lie, "but I think I'm just going to talk from the heart, instead." I lay the notebook on the pulpit.

Heads nod in support.

"When I heard my dad died," I say, "I thought I knew exactly what that meant. But I started to realize that maybe I didn't know my dad as well as I thought I did. Or, I mean, not that I didn't know him, but there's so much more to him than I ever knew. The way he was at home with me and with my mom and my sister," I motion at the front row, "was just a part of the whole."

Everybody just stares at me, their eyes unreadable.

"My dad," I say. "He was a very different sort of man, when I look at the bigger picture, than I had thought. You know, as his son. And I think I realized more than anything these past two days just how real he was. He wasn't just my dad. He was much more than that."

I look at Lillian and my mom in the front row. "All I can say is that I wish I could have known him better. Understood him more fully."

They look up at me, the people in the sanctuary, and with their heads cocked and their eyes shiny and moist, they all look like lost children. I wonder if this is what Pastor Nathan sees every Sunday, if this is how we all look from the pulpit.

"All I'll ever really know him as is who he was with me," I say. "He loved me, and I guess really that's all that should matter."

All I have is a minute or two, a little bit of quiet before I have to go back downstairs to the reception. Everybody will want to talk to me, to shake my hand and tell me how sorry they are about my dad, how proud they're sure he was of me. And in this minute or two, which I managed to steal by telling my mom that my shirt was sweaty from carrying the coffin and that I needed to pop upstairs and change, I don't want to think about anything. I just want silence.

But instead my mind keeps running over the fact that a minute goes by quickly, that my mom is probably keeping her eye on the clock downstairs and greeting people as they enter, telling them that I'll be down soon and she's sure I'd love to see them. I'm lying here on my bed in my white undershirt and staring up at the ceiling, trying not to glance at the clock myself.

I don't want to think about the funeral or the burial service. About Pastor Nathan standing by the long black hearse with the back doors swung open. The throng of people gathered around the gravesite. The heft of the coffin bearing down on my shoulders. The steady march behind Pastor Nathan, who walked with his head tilted down as though in prayer. I don't want to think about it, but I do.

As I walked behind Pastor Nathan, I looked at the ground and watched his shiny black shoes, which peeked out beneath his robe and trampled the brown grass in front of him. But the grass, already old and withered and barely alive this time of year, kept springing back up after each step Pastor Nathan took. It didn't reach quite as high as it did before, but it didn't stay pressed against the ground either. Then I stepped on it, flattened it against the ground again, and wondered if behind me, it still lifted up.

My muscles ache and I'm exhausted. The coffin was even heavier than I had imagined. What I'd really like to do right now is just fall asleep. Ignore the gathering clamor of the reception downstairs, climb under the store-bought patchwork quilt and close my eyes.

But even if I did, it wouldn't make any difference. I would just wake up in an hour or two and have to face it all anyway. These things, they don't just go away. Nothing ever just goes away.

My cell phone rings, and I pick it up, look at Matt's picture on the screen. I haven't even spoken to him since I've been back in Harsville, and he feels so far away. He doesn't even know that the funeral was today. He's really the only person in the world that I want to talk to right now, but just as I'm about to answer his call I hear a light tapping on my door and look up to see Lillian swinging the door open.

"Hi," she says. "Mom said to come check on you."

I toss my phone on the bed beside me. "I was just going to change."

She steps inside. "It's weird, seeing it like this," she says. "Like it's not even your room anymore."

"Well, it isn't," I say. "Not really." My phone beeps to let me know I have a voicemail. I pick it up and look down at it. "You going down?"

"Yeah. I just thought I should . . ." She sighs and walks over to my bed, sits down next to me. "How are you doing?" She nudges me with her shoulder.

"I guess I'm holding up okay. I mean, it's natural to feel sad at your dad's funeral, right?"

She slips her arm around me and gives me a tight, sideways hug.

"But, you know," I say, but I don't know how to go on from there.

"What do I know?" she asks.

"Lillian," I say and then stop. "Lillian," I say again, but still nothing comes.

She starts rubbing my shoulder. "What's going on?"

I take a deep breath and squeeze my eyes shut. "I'm gay," I say, and for a moment, I think my heart stops beating.

I expect there to be a pause, but there is no discernable change in her expression and she keeps rubbing my shoulder as though I didn't say anything at all.

"I'm gay," I say again, "and Dad knew."

"So I'm the only person you didn't trust enough to tell?"

I shake my head. "He just sort of found out. This is the first time I've even said it out loud." I laugh. "I'm not even sure if my boyfriend knows."

"Ah-ha," she says and stops rubbing my shoulder to poke me in the side. "So there's a boyfriend."

I blush in spite of myself. "His name is Matt."

"Shit, Timothy, I had no idea."

I nod. "I'm in love."

"That's great. You should have brought him to the funeral. That would have been fun." She laughs.

I laugh, too. Suddenly it doesn't feel like such a big thing. Suddenly it feels like the most natural thing in the world: love. "Dad showed up unannounced at my dorm a couple weeks ago. Found us, you know, asleep together."

"Oh man." Lillian stands up and faces me. "But you know what, though? *You* are a pretty amazing human being."

I furrow my brow. "Where did that come from?"

"I don't know. I just wish I could be as forgiving as you." She walks to the door. "You coming?"

"Be down in a sec."

She closes the door behind her, and I pull up my voice-mail and press the phone against my ear. "Hey, Timmy B. Just wanted to check in. See how you're doing. I, uh, haven't heard from you, so I just thought I'd call. I'm so sorry about your dad. I hope everything's going okay." A pause, and then, "I love you. Give me a call just, you know, just whenever. I miss you. Bye."

When I call him back, he answers almost immediately, halfway through the first staticky ring. "Hey."

"Hey," I say, and realize that, since my dad's death, this is the first time I feel like I'm about to cry.

"How are you?"

I take a deep breath and steady myself. "Good. I'm sorry I haven't called. Everything's been so crazy down here."

"I can imagine. You holding up okay?"

"Yeah," I say. "The funeral was today."

"Oh yeah? Want to talk about it?"

"Yeah," I say, "but I can't right now. I have to go to the reception. I just wanted to call and hear your voice for a second."

He laughs. "It's good to hear your voice, too."

"I've gotta get down there, but hey, I'll call you after, okay?"

"No worries," he says. "Spend time with your family. See you when you get home."

"Okay. I miss you," I say. "I love you."

"I love you, too."

I hang up and toss the phone on my bed, then walk to my closet, pull out a crisp shirt and put it on over my undershirt. I pause at the top of the stairs to gauge my reflection in the glass that covers one of the pictures on the wall. I try to smooth my hair back with the palms of my hands, then refocus my eyes on the picture itself. Me in my cap and gown at my graduation from the Academy. Smiling, I'm holding the diploma up with one hand, pumping a fist in the air with the other. I remember that feeling, relief at having finished mixed with a delirious kind of hope. Expectation of what was to come. College. Med school. A long and rewarding career as a neurologist. Not knowing what else was to come, too. Confusion. Doubt. Love. And my dad's death, less than a year away.

My mom's voice drifts up from the living room below. "Timothy? You coming down?"

"I'm on my way." But before I turn to walk down the stairs, I take one last glimpse of the picture and try my best to look like the same Timothy as the one made of ink and heavy paper, safely encased behind a pane of glass.

THANK YOU AND GOD BLESS

I tried to get out of dinner. Told Candace I was sick. "If you think I'm going to April's without you," she said. "She's not *my* sister," she added.

"Well, legally," I said.

She handed me my keys.

Down Front Street, I blasted the air conditioner. Candace didn't try to turn it down, or even say, "Greg," in that way she has, which I took as a sort of apology. I fiddled with my phone to find a song. I wanted something dark, some doom, maybe, or better yet, drone. I settled on a song by Earth and slid my phone between my right thigh and the seat.

She adjusted the volume a little. "You gonna say anything to her?"

"No. I'm just going to eat and leave without saying anything the whole time." I turned the volume back up again, just a little.

Candace sighed. "You know what I mean."

"Are *you* going to say anything to her?"

"I'm not the one who saw it," she said, like somehow the seeing was the thing, not the knowing, like if she had been the one running to the pharmacy that day, she'd hold herself responsible to tell my sister. But that was bullshit. Candace didn't even like April, and April didn't like Candace much. The chances of them having a meaningful conversation about anything, let alone April's jackass of a husband, seemed about as likely as me having a heart-to-heart with Griff about what I'd seen.

"None of my business anyway." I hammered the drum beat against the steering wheel. Why did I pick Earth? This song was too slow. I wanted something more aggressive, angry. "Or yours."

April's apartment was too hot, as always. You might think the heat results from four people crammed into a two bedroom with the tiniest kitchen you've ever seen, but you'd be wrong. Griff keeps the heat blasting year round. When the boys were babies, I used to worry what it might do to them. When I would hold them, their hair was always matted to their head with sweat. Now, they're all old enough, they're used to it, even seem to like it. When they come to my house, they think it's too cold, think my house is too big, the dinnerware too fragile. I told Candace once that the best thing we can do for those kids is show them by example how much better it can be, that hard work and an education can get you more in life than a crappy third-floor apartment in a neighborhood that always seems to be on the local news. Never seemed to get through to them, though. Ryan asked me once, "Are you rich or something?" and when I told him, "No," I tried to imbue the word with significance. He just grunted and said, "'Cause you got a lot of pointless stuff" and tilted his head at our curio cabinet.

So the heat was blasting, and the table was maybe a foot away from the oven—another thing that's always made me nervous for the boys—and Griff was nowhere in sight. "I made pot pie," April said.

"Smells delicious." Candace pulled off her jacket and hugged April. Candace insisted on hugging everyone every time she said hello or goodbye. April and I didn't come from a touchy-feely family like that, and I'd warned Candace once: "You're making April uncomfortable," but she'd shrugged it off.

It made me uncomfortable too, but I didn't tell Candace that. If Candace hugged someone, I felt obligated to do it too. I leaned into April and gave her shoulder a squeeze. "Thanks for having us," I said. I handed her the bottle of Cabernet Sauvignon we'd brought.

April looked at it like she didn't know what it was, even though I bring a bottle of wine every time.

Ryan and Markie led Candace into the living room. They were playing some video game that seemed too violent, at least for Markie. He's only seven, although you wouldn't know it, the things you hear coming out of his mouth sometimes. Ryan's ten, and although ten is pretty young too, I remember the things I was responsible for at that age and can appreciate that he sees himself as a kind of almost-adult. When we come over, Markie and Ryan always try to sequester Candace as quickly as they can, which is fine with Candace—she loves those kids—but it always bothers me a little. It means I'm left alone to figure out how to make conversation with April and Griff. April and I share almost nothing anymore besides a tenuous connection to the past, memories of elaborate childhood play, the elf Gregorious and the fairy princess Aprilium, questing for fortune and battling the savage Leviathan. Saturday mornings, sneaking past the couch where our dad slept under a mound of tattered quilts. If we woke him, we ran, giggling, to the basement, where we would regroup and form a new plan. And then, after he left, weekday mornings spent getting ready for school together, me pouring April her cereal, forging our mom's signature on the daily behavior calendar April's teacher sent home because our mom worked late and slept late and didn't have much energy for parenting in-between. We used to be so close, April and I. Sometimes I try to trace where we went wrong. I don't remember growing apart, only just one day, realizing that we had, that

April had a life and I had a life and neither one of us played a very big role in the other's.

Griff and I have less in common. We have only April.

"Should we open this guy up?" I asked, tilting my head to the wine.

April handed it back to me. "You can. I'm off alcohol for the moment."

I turned away to fish through the utensil drawer for a corkscrew. Off alcohol for the moment could only mean one thing: April was pregnant again. My hands felt trembly. I found the corkscrew but pretended to search a bit longer to steady my hands before turning back. "Off alcohol?" I asked. "More for me, I guess."

April shrugged. "I guess so." She reached into a cupboard and pulled out a plastic cup, the kind you get with a kid's meal at a diner, and handed it to me.

"What, no clean sippy cups?"

"Unless you'd rather just drink from the bottle." She put the cup on the counter in front of me. She stepped around me and slipped a burnt oven mitt over her right hand to retrieve the pot pie from the oven.

I filled the cup with wine, drained it, and refilled it. I didn't usually drink that much that quickly, and I felt it hit pretty quick. Tension in my shoulders released, and I leaned back against the counter.

April announced that the food was ready and that we didn't need to wait for Griff. He would be back later.

"How's his job hunt going?" Candace asked, seating herself between Markie and Ryan at the table.

April shook her head. "The job market's still in the shitter."

Candace glanced at Markie, but he was busy mounding mashed potatoes on top of his piece of pie and didn't seem to notice his mom's language, not that it would have meant anything to him anyway. He hears worse from Griff on a daily basis.

Still, Candace never ceases to be shocked when she hears April curse in front of the boys. When Markie looked up from his plate, Candace covered her ears and crossed her eyes. Markie laughed.

"Pretty much everyone outsources anymore," April said.

I swirled the wine around in my cup, the way I've seen sommeliers do, and took a deep sip, and then another. "Is he still answering phones at that warehouse?" I asked, then emptied the cup and refilled it before sitting at the table.

"For now," April said, looking at Candace. "But they don't even have full-time hours. He has to take what he can get."

"Yeah, I guess he does," I said. I looked at Candace, tried to catch her gaze so we could exchange a meaningful look. She poured herself some lukewarm tap water from a pitcher in front of her and didn't look at me. "I mean, in this economy? Right?" I took another long sip of wine and spilled a little on my lap. "Shit."

April slid the stack of napkins from the center of the table over to my side of the table without looking at me.

"Maybe you should slow down," Candace said.

"I'm not drunk," I said, dabbing the red spot on my crotch. "I just have an empty stomach is all."

"So eat," April said, still looking at Candace, not me.

Candace took a huge forkful of pot pie into her mouth. She dramatically rolled her eyes back in a show of pleasure. "Yum, yum, yum."

Markie giggled.

"Thanks," April said. "Got the recipe off the back of the bag of peas."

"Peas," Markie said. "I hate peas."

"You're so lucky that your mommy is such a good cook," Candace said in the sickly-sweet voice she uses when she talks to Markie. Like she thinks he's still a baby.

"People spill sometimes. Doesn't mean they're drunk," I said, and took another slow, careful sip of my wine to prove it.

"Nobody said you're drunk, Greg," April said.

"It was implied."

April tossed her fork onto her plate and stared at me. "Nobody even implied it."

"Are you really drunk, Uncle Greg?" Ryan asked.

"Just joking around." I took a bite of April's pot pie. It was kind of bland. She never sets salt and pepper out on the table. She read somewhere it's best not to get kids in the habit, so we all have to suffer.

"Mr. Jeffries says alcohol is poison," Ryan said. "It's basically the same as drinking gasoline." He scooted his chair away from the table and leaned back.

"Eat your pie," April said, motioning her fork at Ryan's plate.

"I'm not an alcoholic, so it's okay for me," I said to Ryan.

"It is?" Ryan poked at his pie crust.

"But Mr. Jeffries is right that children should stay away from alcohol," Candace offered.

"Mr. Jeffries is his teacher," April said, even though we already knew that. Ryan talks about the word of Mr. Jeffries like it's the word of God. I don't remember ever idolizing my teachers like that. It's sweet, I guess, even though it makes me nervous sometimes. What if Ryan ever has a teacher with crazy ideas? Like, what if he has a science teacher someday who tries to tell him evolution isn't real or some bullshit like that?

I turned to April and lifted my cup to her. "To Mr. Jeffries," I said, and took a sip of wine. "So how come you're off gasoline?" I asked April.

April shrugged. "Just a good idea to take a break sometimes." She looked at me.

"I mean, if you have a problem, sure," I said. "But if you're a normal person like you or me, I say drink and be merry."

"If you can hold your alcohol, maybe," April said, looking at Candace again.

"What does it mean to hold alcohol?" Markie asked.

"Your mom is just joking," Candace said. "Both your mom and uncle are just joking." She said it firm and hard.

"All joking aside," I said, "I think your mom has something she wants to tell us. Don't you, April?"

April folded her napkin and placed it on the table. "Such as?"

I put my drink down and tilted my palms toward the ceiling. "Didn't you invite us to tell us something? Don't you have an announcement to make?" April didn't respond, so I continued. "Or are we waiting for Griff, so you can make it together?"

"I don't know what you're talking about," April said.

"Greg," Candace said.

"The pregnancy," I said, looking at Candace.

Candace's eyes widened as she turned to April. "You're having a baby?" Candace looked like she was going to squeal with excitement.

"We're having a baby?" Markie asked. "Is he a boy or a girl? What's his name? When will he be here? Can he sleep in my bed with me?"

April shook her head, her face crimson, her eyes fixed on mine. "I'm not pregnant. We're not having a baby." She placed her fork gently on the table and pushed her chair back. "I'm not drinking," she said slowly, carefully enunciating each word, "because I want to take a break."

I snorted, and a half-chewed pea shot out of my mouth and landed on the table in front of my plate. I ignored it and washed my bite down with a sip of wine. "I got it." I took another sip of wine and stood up to pour the last of the bottle into my cup. "You think I drink too much. You think I'm an alcoholic"

"For fuck's sake," April said.

Candace looked at the boys, then at me. "Greg."

"I didn't say it." I waved my cup in April's direction. Wine sloshed over the edge and dribbled down my wrist.

The front door opened and we could hear Griff's lumbering gait in the hall. He appeared in the kitchen smelling of smoke. He pulled off his ragged Carhartt and slung it over the back of his chair. "Sorry I'm late," he said.

April stood and hugged Griff, kissed him on the cheek.

Candace stood too and hugged him. "How are you?"

"How was work?" April asked, her voice pulled taut.

Griff laughed. "Work was work, you know?" He looked at me. "I mean, nobody really likes work, do they?"

I tilted my head and looked at the remnants of the bottle of wine at the bottom of my cup. I should have brought a second bottle. "Did you have much luck?"

Griff sat down and began piling his plate with potatoes and pie. "Luck?"

"He just answers the phone," April said. "He doesn't make sales calls or anything."

But Griff was looking at me and I was looking at him. It occurred to me that maybe he had seen me that day too. "I guess I got lucky that they didn't ask me to stay late, like they do half the time. This fuckin' loser I work with always clocks in a half hour late, and they always want me to stay and cover him. I mean, just fire him, right? There's gotta be a hundred guys at the unemployment office willing to take his place."

"Or women," Candace agreed.

"Sorry. Yeah. I just meant guys, like, people."

"I thought maybe you were at your other job," I said, still looking directly at Griff.

He stared at me, his expression blank. "I don't have another job."

"Or not job, I guess. Whatever you call it. Vocation."

"Greg," Candace said.

"No, let him finish," April said. "What do you mean, exactly? Griff's other vocation?"

"His other means of making money," I said, and I noticed that I was slurring my words a little. I paused and swallowed hard, then tried again. "The other way he makes money."

Griff and April exchanged a look. "Greg," Griff said in a stern voice. "You got something to say to me, just say it."

I drained the last bit of wine from my cup. "You know what I'm talking about, Griff. You know what I mean."

"You boys all done?" Candace said to the kids, her voice squeaking on the last word. "Maybe you can show me some more of that game."

"Can we, mom?" Ryan asked April.

April nodded, then looked back at Griff.

Griff reached over and took my empty cup from in front of me. "What you drinking there, Greg? Maybe it's time for some water."

"I'm not fucking drunk!"

Griff held his palms out to me. "Alright, buddy. Alright. But maybe it's time for some water, anyway."

"You know what I'm talking about. I saw you." I dabbed the corners of my mouth with my napkin, not because there was anything there, but because I thought it might make me seem collected. "I saw you, Griff."

"Saw me doing what?" Griff asked, still making unwavering eye contact with me.

I sighed. "Do you want to tell April or should I?"

"For fuck's sake," April said. "Griff panhandles sometimes. He has a sign. He doesn't bother anyone. Is that what you're making this whole scene about?"

I felt my left eye twitch.

A smirk pulled at Griff's face. "You didn't think my own wife knew? You either don't think much of my marriage or you don't think much of marriage in general."

"Don't make this about me," I said.

"What business is it of yours if Griff supplements our income a little?" April asked.

"It's illegal," I said, but heard the words slurring again. "Fuck. It is ill-e-gal," I said again. "And it's wrong."

"Why is it wrong?" Griff asked. "I'm not making anyone give me money. If they want to help, they can. If they don't, that's their choice."

"But you have a job."

"A part-time job," April said. "And a family of four to feed."

I turned my attention to April. "So you're okay with this. You don't see anything wrong with it? You're not, I don't know, embarrassed?"

April laughed. "That's what you think I should find embarrassing?" She squeezed her eyes closed and took a deep breath. "Griff isn't the part of my life that embarrasses me."

Suddenly Candace was beside me. "We should probably go." She squeezed my shoulder. "I'm so sorry. He had a long day."

"Don't apologize for me," I slurred.

Candace shook her head. "Thanks for having us."

April called to Markie and Ryan in the living room. "Boys, come say goodbye to your auntie and uncle. They're leaving."

Ryan and Markie came running in to give first Candace, then me a hug. "Will you be okay, Uncle Greg?" Ryan asked me.

"He's fine," Candace said. "I'm driving."

April didn't move, but Griff gave Candace a bear hug. He held his hand out to me and all but crushed my bones in a handshake.

On the drive home, Candace blasted the air conditioner, but closed the vent on the driver's side. The world racing by made me feel dizzy, so I closed my eyes and rested my forehead against the cool glass of the passenger side windowpane. The silence was making my head throb, so I said, "Ridiculous, huh?"

Candace drew in her breath.

"Fucking ridiculous," I said again and relaxed into the gentle vibration of the car. A memory formed in the back of my mind, and I wanted to share it with Candace but my mouth was dry and I couldn't think of how to articulate it. Something about me and April as kids, huddled under the blanket on my bed, trying not to giggle. My dad, pretending to rage about the house as he searched for us: "Fee, Fi, Fo, Fum!" April and I, holding our breath as we peeked out from under the blanket, looking for our dad's shadow.

THE TRUE STORY OF ANNABELLA

But that isn't how it happened at all. I know because I was there. Well, not at the ball, don't be ridiculous. A chicken at a ball. Ha! But I knew the child, Annabella their name was. Wherever did you hear that other name? Settle, now, and listen well. I will tell you how it really went.

Annabella once told me their mother's eyes changed color with her mood. A dark, penetrating blue, like the depths of the ocean, when she was happy; a stormy grey when she was sad. When she found out she was pregnant with Annabella, her eyes had been amethyst, and it was for this reason that Anna's favorite color was purple. Anna used to study their own eyes in the still waters of the koi pond out back, looking for the chameleon gene, some link to the mother they never knew, but Anna's eyes remained a constant sapphire.

That's how we came to be close, Anna and me. They'd spend hours in the yard, talking away to the goats and the rabbits, though those animals didn't have a lick of sense among them, and to the daffodils and the old oak tree. They wasted their babble on those that did not appreciate it, but they talked also, and at great length, to me. They told me romantic tales of their mother and their father in the time before Anna had come to be, and they told me tales of their own exploits, too. Talked of the little twig village they'd built in the forest, beyond my coop's line of sight. Anna said they'd made skyscrapers and bridges and amusement parks and hospitals—all out of mud. They had no dolls that had been manufactured and sold, so they made their own out of branches and rocks they'd scavenged in the forest. It explained their soil blackened fingernails. Poor child, I used to think, whose mother had died in child birth and whose father worked all day as a glass smith and all night tending to the drunks at the tavern. They had no one to clean their hair, to peck the bugs out and smooth the strands.

And that, really, is how I came to take Anna under my wing, which is an expression the humans use, though they do not have wings, as you know. I suppose I thought of Anna as a sort of god-child. What's a godchild? It's another part of human culture. You see, humans have families, just like we chickens, but they extend those families to friends, sometimes, too. A godparent will step in when the biological parent is gone. Anna being motherless, and me having my eggs stolen daily, it just made sense that I should take on that role.

Once, when they were nine, Anna brought me with them to school, stowed inside their knapsack with their books. School is a place human children go to learn the ways of human culture. They are taught things like who won what wars, how to keep track of what they owe to the kingdom, and the names and locations of the different villages near and far. Most of it useless, if you ask me, though I did enjoy when the teacher read to the pupils, even if her stories were far too simplistic, contrived.

I still don't know what possessed Anna to bring me along. The walk to the school grounds was bumpy and dark, and something kept jabbing me. Although they'd left the top of the sack open, the air seemed unbearably thin. Made me long for the confines of my coop, which is something I never thought I'd say. During class, Anna reached in through the top of the sack and patted me, though, which was nice.

Anna brought the sack with me in it to the schoolyard at playtime. I peered through the opening to see that the children were forming small groups—a peep of three, a formation of seven. Anna remained alone on the edge of the grounds, where they plopped down with me in their lap and chattered away to me the way they did at home. I could see the other children watching us. They snickered in that cruel way of humans, whispering to each other and pointing, but Anna paid them no mind.

After a while, a little runt of a girl with pigtails approached Anna and asked them who were they talking to and was it their imaginary friend. Anna reluctantly revealed the top of my head to the little beast, who screamed as though she'd seen a viper. It startled me, the girl's reaction, and I puffed my feathers out and pecked at her hands. She wailed as though she'd been attacked by a bear. I clucked at Anna as the girl galloped across the yard to the teacher. "Well that woman will set her straight," I remember telling Anna, though I'd long since learned that Anna didn't listen, not to me. Imagine my dismay when the teacher came charging over to me and Anna, a look of pure fire on her face. This would be the first of Anna's unmerited expulsions from school.

Anna started at a new school the next week, but like their previous school, they made no friends. If the loneliness bothered Anna, they didn't let on. They spent their afterschool hours in the backyard with me. It was their favorite place to be. The gentle flow of the stream that wound its way along the edge of the property line, the way the light cascaded down the coop's roof and sliced through the shadows—Anna loved it all. We'd talk for hours, them and me, though as I said, Anna loved to talk, not so much to listen. When it came my turn to share my stories, Anna would become distracted, interrupt. I tried to tell Anna how it felt to be literally cooped up, to have your eggs taken from you every day. All I'd ever wanted was to be a mother. But Anna seemed not to understand. I suppose children never do.

On weekends, they would sometimes go with their father to his shoppe to watch him melt and blow glass. They brought me with them once. It was like watching a skillful musician play his instrument, the way he could maneuver the molten mixture into any design he wanted by nimbly twisting and twirling it just so. He would press and prod the glass with his tools and the fluid would magically turn from a mass of nothing into something—a vase, a bowl, a flower, a hairpin. On slow days, he'd let Anna help, and they, too, learned to manipulate the liquid into a work of true beauty.

Anna lived like this for many years: at peace. It wasn't until Anna was fifteen that their world turned upside down. Their father left for work one morning, kissed them on the cheek and told them he loved them, like he did each morning, and then collapsed, dead, on his walk to the glass shoppe. Anna was pulled from school and told the news. They cried, but their tears, they told me later, did not feel like a release.

I held them as best I could—these wings weren't really made for hugging—and tried to soothe them with a story. "When I was a fledgling," I cooed, "my mother was cooked into a stew, and my father was sold to a farmer down the way. I never saw him again. I was sold to your parents, which was lucky because they weren't buying me for meat but for eggs."

Anna rumpled their brow at me, but they laid their head at my feet and let me caress their hair.

Anna and I and the goats and the rabbits were taken in by a new family—a new mother, a father, who sold kitchen wares on the road and was rarely home, and a sister, Margaret. Anna's foster mother preferred to be called Ophelia, not mother or any other endearing term, as she felt it would be unfair to Anna's true mother, may she rest in peace. Anna's new sister was roughly the same age as Anna. Margaret was tall and lean, athletic and popular. She was Anna's exact opposite in every way, and Ophelia encouraged her to be a positive role model for poor, lost Anna, whose hair was often unwashed. "She needs us to show her how to be."

I was taken into the house because they had no coop and, anyway, Ophelia didn't believe it was right, keeping an animal locked away like that. "We are all God's creatures," she said, so I was given free reign of the house and fed from the table. Best of all, I was permitted to sleep in bed with Anna. Ophelia called me her pet, which I think had to do with the way she would caress my feathers after she would finish with the darning in the evenings.

On Wednesdays, Ophelia hosted something she called a Bible study, which Margaret and Anna were required to attend. Ophelia would read from a thick tome, and then she and her guests would discuss it. The stories they read were difficult to decipher sometimes, the language stilted, the character names old-fashioned. They were similar to the stories Anna's teacher read aloud at school, and I enjoyed listening in, though often, Ophelia and her guests' interpretations of the stories lacked nuance and sophistication.

They read, for example, a story about a man who did many great things in his lifetime, saved a multitude of people from slavery, but had difficulty managing his own anger and was, as a result, not permitted entrance into the promised land at the end of the story.

"Nobody's perfect," I clucked.

Ophelia didn't reply and instead scooped me onto her lap and stroked my feathers, which did feel nice, though I was a bit annoyed by her attempt to placate me. The discussion continued as though I hadn't said a thing, and after a moment, I jumped off Ophelia's lap and huffed away, though nobody seemed to care.

Margaret was always quite entranced by the stories and discussions and actively participated—much, it seemed, to Ophelia's satisfaction. Anna, not so much. They would get restless and tap their feet or fiddle with their fingers, and spoke only when directly called upon.

At night, Anna and I would sit by the fire and watch the house cat Francis watch the flames dance. Franny was a fool, like the goats and the rabbits, and would chase me sometimes when no one was looking. I think she meant to make a supper of me. Still, it was amusing watching the way the blaze held her attention. The lack of narrative was beside the point. The constantly shifting light was enough, the capacity for change. Anna told me once they sometimes tried to see what Franny saw in the flickers and flares, tried to imagine themself as the conflagration itself, but could only really understand what it must feel like to be the wood, quietly smoldering.

Sometimes, Margaret would come and sit with us by the fire as she attended to her needlework. Though Margaret and Anna rarely conversed on these occasions, I suspect Anna came to associate Margaret's presence with the warmth of the fire, and in this way, Anna began to silently burn for Margaret. Anna confided in me that they thought of Margaret often. When they lay in bed at night, I'm sure it was Margaret's smile, her laugh, that Anna pictured when they touched themself in the dark, while I pretended not to notice. I imagine Anna wondered what

Margaret's skin felt like to the touch, whether her hair was as silky as it appeared, if her breath tasted like spun sugar.

One day during lunch break at school, Anna witnessed a boy standing close to Margaret, pressing his body against hers and sandwiching her against the brick wall outside the school's auditorium. Anna blushed and started to walk away, but then they heard Margaret's voice, choked with tears and pleading with the boy to stop.

Anna recounted to me how the familiar warmth they always felt when they saw Margaret bloomed inside their belly, and it was followed by heat: rage. Annabella purposefully strode to the boy and grabbed him by the scruff of his neck, the way they would always grab Franny when she would scratch at the furniture or pee on the living room rug. Annabella pulled the boy off of Margaret, then punched the boy square in the nose. Annabella was lean but strong, and the boy howled like a fearful dog.

"Cunts!" he yelled at Anna and Margaret as he pressed his fingers to the gush of blood on his upper lip. "Dykes!"

Margaret didn't thank Anna, just ran to the bathroom alone, but that day on the walk home, Margaret pressed her hand into Anna's. Anna told me that, as they looked at their hands, fingers woven together so that Margaret's were indistinguishable from their own, they resisted the urge to run their thumb over Margaret's soft skin.

When they arrived home, Ophelia was waiting at the door. Margaret dropped Anna's hand. Ophelia told Anna the principal had called, that Anna had been expelled. "I'm not angry," Ophelia said. "Just disappointed."

§

It was shortly after Anna's second expulsion that word spread throughout the land that the prince would be hosting a ball. The purpose of the ball was unstated but clear: the prince wanted to gather all the girls of marrying age in one place, so that he might choose from among them his new bride. It was a common enough practice, and the whole town buzzed with gossip and predictions. Ophelia announced over dinner that night that she would be buying Margaret a new gown, that she had every intention of Margaret winning the prize that was the prince's hand.

"You're pretty enough," she told Margaret, "and pious. If we dress you right and powder your face, the prince won't help but to choose you."

"And Anna?" Margaret asked. "What will Anna wear?"

"Anna won't be in attendance. She's grounded. Or have we already forgotten she assaulted someone?"

Here I feel I should pause and point out that I never understood Ophelia's refusal to call Anna by their preferred pronouns. Gender is another purely human invention. It is based, as far as I can understand, on the assumption that your biological sex affects your behavior, and while I try not to judge, humans seem to me backwards in their binary thinking. Ophelia's insistence on referring to Anna by their biology seemed odd to me. "God doesn't make mistakes," Ophelia would say, but it did not seem to affect Ophelia in the slightest what pronouns Anna wished to use.

Anna chewed their potatoes slowly. They hadn't any interest in attending the ball, but they told me later that the thought of Margaret dancing with the prince gave their stomach an odd twinge.

"I won't go without Anna," Margaret said, folding her napkin and placing it on her plate.

"Besides," Ophelia said, as though Margaret hadn't even spoken, "you don't need the distraction. You need to be unfettered."

"I don't want to marry the prince." Margaret pushed her chair back from the table and stood. "I don't think I will be attending either."

"Sit."

Margaret hesitated, but then obeyed.

"We will shop for your dress tomorrow," Ophelia said.

"Yes, mother," Margaret said.

That night, Anna dreamt of Margaret at the ball. She looked radiant in a dress spun of gold to match her hair, and the prince spent the entirety of the evening spinning and spinning her around the dancefloor. At the end of the dream, the prince kneeled before Margaret. Anna awoke to a pillow wet with tears, and I comforted them 'til dawn.

In the days leading to the ball, Anna talked of little else besides Margaret and the prince. Margaret confessed to Anna that she didn't like the prince much, didn't find him attractive, for one thing, and didn't agree with his policies. "He's spoiled," Margaret said by the fire one night, "and only cares for his kind. You've seen the poverty in our streets, the sick who can't afford medicine, the starving who can't afford food. He could change that, but he doesn't."

Anna nodded. Though politics held little interest for them, they couldn't deny that the prince seemed to do little for the people in his kingdom, just like his father before him. Marrying such a cad would indeed be unpleasant, but more than anything, I think Anna felt relieved that Margaret hadn't fallen prey to the prince's overt charms—his good looks and muscular body, and his moody brown eyes that drew so many of the kingdom's young women in.

"I wish you could go with me," Margaret told Anna. "It wouldn't be so awful if you were there."

And this is how Anna resolved to attend the ball, in spite of Ophelia's directive otherwise. They must be there for Margaret, they told me, and they began collecting scraps from Ophelia's sewing room to piece together a makeshift gown. They stayed up late into the night and hand-stitched the fabric together.

One afternoon after finishing their chores, Anna took me to their father's vacant shoppe to fashion a pair of slippers from glass, deftly twirling and shaping the liquid into a delicate but sturdy pair of flats. They admitted to me the slippers pinched their toes and were too hard against the bottoms of their feet, but oh how the glass shimmered in the sunlight. It would just be one night, Anna said, and they could bear the pain for Margaret.

When Anna wriggled the gown over their head and slid the slippers on their feet, something magical happened. They seemed to transform into someone new, someone beautiful and unrecognizable. Anna had washed up in preparation, and powdered their face and rouged their cheeks in an attempt to not stand out. Now, with the gown hugging their waist and hips, Anna looked stunning. In the looking glass that evening, Anna finally saw a glimpse of their mother looking back. No one would recognize them, I assured Anna. And I was right: no one did. No one, that is, but Margaret, who looked deeply into Anna's sapphire eyes and knew them at once.

The next part of the story you know. They went to the ball; they danced. But the version of the story you've heard isn't true. The prince tells it like this: a mysterious, elegant woman appeared, danced with him, and won his favor. That's only partly accurate. Anna was mysterious and elegant, indeed, and they won the prince's admiration, if only for aesthetic reasons. But Anna did not dance a single waltz with the prince. Anna spent the evening dancing with Margaret, or huddled by the food table and whispering with Margaret, or out on the veranda, identifying constellations with Margaret. At no point that night did Anna engage with the prince in any way, and so it must have come as quite a surprise when the prince made his formal announcement at the end of the night: the woman in the patchwork gown would be his new bride.

Everyone at the ball turned to look at Anna, whose heart, I can imagine, drummed an unsteady rhythm. The prince stood before the throne and stretched his arm out toward them. Anna's palms slickened as they reached for Margaret's hand, but Margaret folded her own hands into each other and looked down. And that's when Anna ran. It wasn't so much a decision as an instinct. The stiff glass of the slippers made running difficult, so Anna kicked off their shoes one at a time before racing down the front steps of the castle. One slipper clattered down the stairs and shattered against the cement below, but the other came to rest in the soil of a tulip bed beside the front gate.

And you know what happened next: the prince diverted resources that could have been used elsewhere to search for the mysterious maiden. No expense was spared, and anyone with information about the identity of the woman was to come forward or risk imprisonment. Those first few days, some women came forward claiming to be the one, but none were able to fit into the unbroken slipper, and they were each summarily put to death for perjury.

For several days after the ball, Anna couldn't eat. They slept fitfully at night, waking every time I ruffled my feathers. The anxiety that consumed them was not so much about getting caught as it was about Margaret's safety. Margaret vowed to Anna that she wouldn't turn them in, but Anna didn't like the position they'd put Margaret in. Anna wished that they could undo the entire night. Why had they insisted on attending the ball, anyway? Why had they let jealousy get the better of them?

A week into the prince's search, Anna grabbed the dress they'd worn to the ball and whispered me awake. They told me their plan: they were leaving. They couldn't put Margaret in danger any longer. They would drown the dress in the river, then head west and start a new life.

"Take me with you," I squawked, but as usual, Anna didn't listen.

I followed Anna as they stepped down the hall and into Margaret's room. They sat on the edge of the bed and smoothed Margaret's hair over her forehead.

Margaret stirred and looked at Anna, smiled. "It's you. I was just dreaming about you."

"Margaret," Anna whispered, "I'm leaving. I can't risk you getting found out."

Margaret squeezed Anna's hands. "We will run away together." Margaret slid a strand of Anna's hair behind their ear.

Anna blushed. "I can't ask that of you."

"You haven't." Margaret stood. "I'm coming with you because I choose to. I'm coming with you because I want to be with you."

Anna looked down at the floor. "I feel," they said, "like this is a prank. Like you're going to turn on me and tell me everything I am is wrong. It's how everyone else feels. Or maybe you're just going to leave me to die. Like my mother left. Like my father."

"I would never hurt you like that. I couldn't." Margaret reached for Anna's hands again. Anna lifted Margaret's knuckles to their lips and kissed them, one at a time. "Margaret," Anna said at last, "you're the only one besides my father who ever showed me love."

"Well!" I said from the doorway, but they didn't seem to hear.

"I do love you." Margaret leaned forward. "I love you, Anna. I do."

Anna kissed Margaret. Margaret's lips were chapped and parted slightly as they pressed back against Anna's. Anna held Margaret as close as they possibly could, pressing their body against hers.

The next morning, Ophelia found them together, tangled in Margaret's sheets. She saw Anna's wrinkled ball gown on the floor. "You're the one," she cried. "It's you." Ophelia clasped her fingers around Anna's wrist and pulled.

Margaret clawed at the back of her mother's hand. "Let them go," she said.

Ophelia wrenched back and straightened her nightgown. "You have disgraced this house," she said to Anna. "I took you in, trusted you. I should have known you were wicked all along."

Ophelia spoke to Anna, but it was Margaret who replied. "It is you who are wicked, mother. You are the one who is a disgrace."

Ophelia slapped Margaret, hard. Margaret reeled back and pressed her fingers to her cheek. "I will call the castle guards. I will tell them what I know."

"If you call the guards, they will arrest Margaret," Anna said. "Would you do this to your own daughter?"

Ophelia didn't respond.

"We will leave." Anna stood. They held their hand out to help Margaret up too, but Margaret did not take it.

"Come to your senses then?" Ophelia asked.

"She doesn't need you to tell her who she is," Anna said.

Margaret looked at Anna's extended hand, then at her mother. She opened her mouth as if to speak, but no words came out.

Anna dropped their hand to their side and looked pleadingly at Margaret.

Margaret looked down, scrunched the sheets between her fingers.

"Margaret," Anna said.

Ophelia stepped to Margaret's wardrobe and pulled an old, brown dress from a hanger. She tossed it at Anna. "Cover yourself."

Anna looked down at their exposed body. They slipped the dress quickly over their head, then turned again to Margaret. "Will you go with me?" they asked.

Margaret pressed her lips together.

Ophelia laughed. "She's a good child. She was led astray."

"Led astray my feathers," I squawked.

Ophelia lifted me into her arms.

I flapped my wings to free myself, but she tightened her hold on me. I pecked at her fingers and arms, and when she dropped me, I scurried after Anna, who was already halfway down the front path. I called after them, but they did not look back. They did not need me anymore. Perhaps they never had.

So the story came to a close thus, with Ophelia standing by the door and Margaret lifting the blanket around her naked body in bed. I've heard tell that Anna made it safely to a mountain village far away, where they settled and married and lived happily the rest of their days, but of those details, I know very little. Though Ophelia had always been kind to me, I ran away that morning too. I couldn't stand to live in that house any longer, not after how Ophelia had treated Anna. All I can tell you is that the prince didn't find them, and Ophelia never called the guards, and the version of the story the prince tells, about the woman he eventually did marry, the one he found whose foot fit the slipper, is not the true story.

The true story is much more complicated and messy. The truth is Anna never needed a prince or fairy godmother, and Margaret wasn't ugly, on the inside or out, just afraid. I'd like to tell you that one day, many years later, Margaret found love, that

Margaret stood up to Ophelia, that Ophelia learned a lesson and changed. But these things aren't the truth either. True stories are filled with unhappy endings, after all, or endings that are only happy enough. What I can tell you is that Anna most certainly forgave Margaret. I'd like to believe Margaret one day forgave herself.

And I can tell you, also, that Anna carried nothing with them that morning as they disappeared into the forest. The breeze brought with it early morning birdsong, and though there was a slight chill to the air and the dress Anna wore was threadbare, Anna did not wrap their arms around themself. As they strode into the forest, their arms swayed gently at their sides, and their face lifted to the sun.

FIRST SNOW

Jay is driving way too fast. The trees and bushes and perfectly maintained lawns are flying by. I know I should tell him to slow down, that there is a baby in the car and this behavior is not okay. He would say to look who's talking. I can't get into it with him, not right now. It's snowing—big, fluffy flakes that just melt into the asphalt—and it's like the headlights are illuminating a world of stars, like we're racing through the vacuum of space and not a residential subdivision at three in the morning.

Meggie's silence, after four hours of non-stop wailing, makes me feel unhinged. It blends with the stillness of the streets and the snowfall, the void of this suburb, which had seemed so inviting and friendly when we were first looking at the house, the kind of place where your neighbors will call you by name when they see you working in your garden. I don't know how to garden, but four months ago, pregnant with Meggie and with hope, everything seemed possible. We've been living in the house for a month now, and I don't know any of our neighbors' names. One of them, the middle-aged man in the house to the left of ours, waved at me, once, as he mowed his lawn, but that's as close as we've come to the 1950's life I'd imagined for us here.

Our yard is an unkempt mess of weeds and overgrown grass, and our garage is still home to too many unpacked boxes.

Now, as we rocket down the streets in the dark and through the snow, the neighborhood feels sinister. Meggie feels that way to me too, sometimes. When I look in her eyes, I think there should be something there—love, recognition, some sign that she is human. But she seems to feel none of those things, just want and need and discontent, not really feelings at all, if you think about it, but animal instincts, impulses unattached to forethought or reflection.

The strap of the seatbelt presses into my breasts, which are uncomfortably heavy with milk, and I squirm, try to reposition myself without disturbing Meggie, whose little hand clutches tightly to my index finger. Meggie can usually smell my milk from the other side of the house. It drives her crazy, the smell. She's like an addict. But right now, I can't stomach the idea of her relentless sucking, the way she keeps at it until she's drained me and then needs more just an hour later. I spend 12 hours a day breastfeeding; I logged it one time in my journal just to check.

Jay stops at the corner of Elm and Birch, then clears his throat and reaches back for my hand—at least that's what I assume he's grasping for, but I can't say for sure because I don't reach forward. His hand is shaking slightly. Could be from the jostling of the car's engine, which has something wrong with it—I've been telling Jay for weeks. Or could be something else. He examines me through the rearview mirror, and his eyes look the same—dark and cloudy and pleading and lost—as they did that day he first told me he loved me seven years ago. He said it slowly, pronounced each syllable like he was speaking to a foreigner, and he sandwiched it with my name: "Beth, I love you, Beth." I'd been caught off guard—by all of it, really, but especially by hearing my name twice in the same sentence. It shot me back to my childhood, to playing in the muddy shallows of the creek after my mom had expressly told me not to, to my mom's rage as she stuttered my name too many times to count, so filled with disappointment she couldn't even figure out where to go after "Beth." The fear I felt then is the same sort of fear I felt as Jay searched my face for some sort of reaction, the way his eyes darted from my left eye to my right as he waited for me to reciprocate. It had all seemed to span hours at the time, but I know it couldn't have been more than a few seconds. I could tell, even as my mind turned over the possible replies trying to find the one that felt true, that I was taking too long to respond.

He reaches forward and pushes the button to turn on the hazard lights, then drops his hand to the armrest, his elbow jutting back so I can reach forward and squeeze it if I want, but I don't. The strobing of the hazard lights paints the fresh snow amber.

"She asleep?" Jay asks.

I look at Meggie. "I don't know," I say, even though I'm pretty sure she is. Her head is just sort of lolling against the side of the car seat, and her hand feels limp in mine. "I don't think I really know how to tell."

Jay sighs theatrically and turns off the hazards, pressing the button with unnecessary force. "Whatever," he mumbles as he pulls his hand back to the steering wheel and speeds through the intersection, turning left instead of right, which would have led us home.

His frustration frustrates me, but I'm so sick of arguing. I don't even remember the last time we argued before the birth. Surely we'd had arguments before, but I can't seem to remember a single one, and I know, anyway, that they were nothing like they are now, that kind of argument where you end up not talking for hours, the kind where you're still so mad after it's over that you don't even want to cry. I told my mom a few days ago about the fights, about how frequent they're becoming, how fierce. I brought it up casually, and maybe that was my mistake. Maybe she didn't understand it was a cry for help, my telling her.

All she did was laugh and tell me it was sleep deprivation. I tried to tell her it seemed like more, but she just told me, again, about the time she came this close to stabbing my dad in the thigh with knitting needles, then changed the subject back to Meggie. "Have her eyes turned color yet? Is her hair coming in?"

A better question would have been, "Do you feel like her mother yet?" My mom never says the right thing.

Jay taps his wedding ring against the steering wheel, a habit he's had ever since the first day I slipped the ring on his finger, and I'm afraid the soft, discordant knocking is going to wake Meggie, but I don't say so. We zoom wordlessly past Maple and Beechwood and Forest, then make another left on Flora Avenue before I look at Jay and say, in a half-whisper so I won't wake Meggie, "I didn't mean it," but I did, and he knows it, so I add, "I mean I guess I did, in the moment, but I don't mean it anymore."

He stops tapping his ring but doesn't say anything, just like he didn't say anything earlier tonight, when I held Meggie out to him with one hand, her tensed body rolled into a ball, quaking with the power of each howl. I knew my hold on her was tenuous, that one good shriek might cause my grip to fail, but I knew, also, that Jay would hurry over, would grab her before she fell and hug her tightly to his chest as though he were the one, not me, responsible for nursing her.

And that's when I'd said it, what no mother is ever supposed to say. And it's not like I'd thought about it, run the words through my filter and decided to say them after carefully working out how Jay might respond, but still, I hadn't expected the response I got: Jay, grabbing Meggie from me like he thought I might do her harm, turning his back on me as he cradled and hummed and whispered who knows what in her ear.

Jay'd always been strangely suspicious of me, even back when I was pregnant. He'd asked our midwife, Sue, during an appointment once whether someone who was prone to depression was more likely to get post-partum depression, and if so, might that someone be likely to hurt the baby.

Sue'd hesitated before reaching forward and squeezing my knee and saying, "You just need to watch for the signs."

I'd appreciated the sympathy in her eyes, but I was so mad at Jay for bringing it up, so casual like that. "I'm not going to hurt my own baby," I told him on the drive home from the appointment. I didn't look at him as I said it, just stared out the passenger side window, one hand on my belly, the other on the seatbelt strap trying to keep it slack.

"I know," he told me. "I was just running through the possibilities." Such a passive-aggressive way of diverting the fact that he'd just implied in front of our midwife that he believed I might pose a threat to my own child.

I wonder, now, if he still feels that way, if he thinks I'm going to hurt Meggie. I'm not. I might not be the best mother in the world, but if anyone, the one I might hurt is myself. "I don't wish we never had Meggie," I say, and still, Jay says nothing, offers no reprieve. This silence suddenly feels like the worst silence so far, and I have to say something to keep myself from saying everything. "It's just, sometimes it's harder than I thought, you know? Sometimes I wonder if the whole thing about loving your kid instantly, about that motherly bond, sometimes I wonder if it's all just bullshit."

I don't know what I expect—an epiphanic moment, I guess, some indication that he understands, at last—but instead, here's what I get: his fingers, wrapped loosely around the steering wheel, slightly tighten; his jaw tenses, then immediately relaxes; he says nothing, keeps hurtling through the night, dragging me and Meggie along with him.

Meggie begins to cough beside me, that deep, throaty kind her pediatrician doesn't know what to do about, and her eyes fly open and she lets out a quick cry. My body reacts, and my painfully full breasts begin to leak. Two deep circles of wetness form where my nipples meet my shirt, and I pull my hand away from Meggie's and use it to reposition the fabric against my chest. Luckily, Meggie doesn't seem to mind. Her eyelids have already drifted back down, and she's moaning slightly, but she seems to be out.

I look in the rearview mirror and see Jay watching me. His eyes dart back to the road right away, but it's too late: I'm blushing—not because I feel shy about how overstated my breasts must look right now or the way the gathering wetness is drawing attention to them, but because of the way I drew away from my own child right when my body was telling me to nurture her. "I'm sore," I say, and rub the wet spots to prove it, but I'm not even sure if he hears me because I say it so quietly. He doesn't respond.

I look back down at Meggie, run my fingers over the soft plumpness of her cheeks, her thin lips so much like mine, but I feel nothing, and nothing, and nothing still, no matter how hard I try. She's definitely in a deep sleep now. She's doing that sucking thing, like even in her dreams, all she cares to do is draw the life out of me. I'm about to tap Jay on the shoulder, whisper to him that she's out, that we can go home, when my body flings itself against the seatbelt. Meggie's slams against the back of her rear-facing car seat. The thud is short-lived and replaced almost immediately by the sound of Jay's keys dangling in the ignition, Jay turning the hazard lights back on, and the slow, rhythmic click of the lights flashing on and off.

I look at Meggie and am surprised to see that she's still asleep. It seems impossible, but after everything tonight, she's fallen into a deep enough sleep that a car accident hasn't even roused her.

Jay drops his head to the steering wheel. As if of its own volition, my hand reaches forward and squeezes his shoulder.

He looks up and twists around to see me. "Meggie okay? You okay?"

"We're fine. What happened?"

"Fuck," he mumbles to himself. He undoes his seatbelt and climbs out of the car, leaving me no choice but to follow.

On the road in front of the car is a crumpled body. At first, I think it's a human body—the dark brown looks like hair, not fur, and it's matted with blood. Then I recognize it: it's the poodle I've seen around the neighborhood—a standard poodle, not a toy. I don't know its name, or its owners' names, or where they live, or why they would have let their dog run loose in the middle of the night. Its eyes are open and unmoving; its little neck, twisted and splintered with bone. I fight the urge to look away because something inside me tells me to step forward, that I have to see this, have to acknowledge it for what it is.

Jay kneels down beside the dog and places his hand on its exposed belly. "I didn't see it," he says.

"I know."

"I mean, it just appeared. It wasn't there, and then it was."

"I know," I say again, and I do. The snow is melting into the dog's fur, and I think for a moment how cold it must feel, even though I know it doesn't feel anything anymore.

Jay leans down and feels for a tag, but there's nothing. No collar or anything. "Where'd it come from?" Jay asks, standing up and looking into the wooded thicket beside the road.

I shrug.

Jay looks back down at the dog. "Must be a stray."

"Maybe," I say to make him feel better.

We watch the snow blanket the dog with a moist sheen, and then suddenly, Jay looks at me and says, "I know you didn't mean it." It's a lie, I can see it in his eyes, but maybe some lies are necessary. "I know you love her; I know you do." I don't say anything, and he adds, softly, as though he's speaking to the dog, "We both love her," and the way he says it—I don't know, it's like he's trying to persuade himself.

I reach out and take Jay's hand. His palm is sweaty and warm—strange, because it's so cold tonight, and yet the strangeness is comforting. At first, his hand is lifeless in mine, and I wonder if my concession comes too late, but then he starts to stroke my knuckles with his thumb. "What do we do?" I nod toward the dog.

Jay shakes his head and looks back over his shoulder at the car, at Meggie's car seat. "I don't even know what you're supposed to do in this kind of," but his voice chokes and gives out before he can finish.

I squeeze his hand and rest my head on his shoulder. The world around me is cold, but Jay's neck is warm, and I burrow my nose into it, breathing in his sweat and the ghost of his aftershave. "It's okay," I say into his skin. "I don't think anybody really knows what to do."

And then we stand there saying nothing, letting the sound of the wind and the snow and the empty streets enclose us, sing us its own lullaby. This must be the sound that lulled Meggie to sleep in the car. It's somehow the sound of nothing and everything all at once, and it's beautiful in its complete meaninglessness.

I don't know how long we stand there, warming each other, before Jay pulls back and tells me, "Come on. Let's get Meggie home."

"What are we going to do about," and I motion to the dog.

He shrugs. "Can you help me move it off the road?"

I nod and step over to the dog, bend down and feel its warmth, which still has yet to dissipate. It's heavier than I would have thought, but between the two of us, Jay and I are able to drag it to the edge of the road. When I climb in the front passenger seat of the car, the shock of warmth from the heater feels stifling. I reach forward to turn it off, but then look over my shoulder at the back of Meggie's car seat and stop myself. Jay slowly pulls away from the dog and we drive in silence home.

When we get there, Jay carries Meggie to her room and slides her into the crib. I climb into bed alone. The sheets are freezing. I curl my legs up and curve my body into them, wait for Jay to climb into bed beside me and click off the lamp, so we can lie here side by side in the cold.

BUBBLE

Jess is wearing that sweater I like, the green one that matches her seafoam eyes. It's taking all of my willpower to keep myself from telling her how pretty she looks. I could play it off as a female thing—one woman empowering another or whatever—but Ryan is already suspicious, Jess says, and we have to be more careful. And anyway, I'm not in the mood for Ryan's homophobic humor right now, not that I ever am. It's Saturday, and I'm exhausted from another week of Zoom. I just want to relax, have fun.

Her bangles spin around her delicate wrist as she lifts her wine glass. "Cheers to breaking the law."

We stand up and clink our drinks and then take a sip. Whether it's the pregaming, or the release from a long week, maybe the sight of Jess's glossy lips as she takes a drink, I feel almost giddy as the wine washes over my tongue. I laugh, and everyone looks at me. "Sorry," I say. "It's just funny. You know? *Breaking the law.*"

"Amanda's right," Geoff says. "We oughta be more careful." He steps to the window and peaks through the crack between the curtains.

"Ryan might be working undercover right now," I say.

Ryan grabs Geoff's wrists and pretends to handcuff him, which is Ryan's go-to move when someone jokes about him being a cop.

"I don't know about you guys, but I've been looking forward to tonight all week," Jess says.

She doesn't look at me as she says it, but I know I'm the one she's been waiting to see, and I take another finger of wine to hide my smile.

"We're so glad we have you guys," Ryan says. "Glad you're not afraid to get together like this."

We cheers again before sitting back down—Jess, Ryan, and me on the couch, Geoff on the easy chair.

"Same," Geoff says. "I mean, we already spend time with the people we live with. What's the difference if you extend that to a few people outside of your house?"

It's a bubble, or a pod. That's how I describe it to my sister, anyway, when we do our Facetime check-ins. Really, it's an excuse to hang out. I know it even when I say it—"my quaranteam," I call them, and the word tastes sour because I know it's a lie, or at least, it's not all of the truth. The whole truth is Ryan still works outside of the house, and neither of them are taking the pandemic very seriously.

It's just, it was too fucking lonely, those first few weeks in lockdown. We were going crazy, me and Geoff, trapped in the house together, just us two. Cabin fever doesn't even come close. His voice is different when he Zooms in to work. He changes. And he leaves dishes lying around, and he wears a button-up shirt with basketball shorts and Adidas slides. That sort of thing. We were probably at risk of divorce if we hadn't agreed that we couldn't take it anymore; we had to get together with *someone*, lockdown be damned. It just happened Ryan and Jess felt the same.

"I'd go crazy if I didn't have you guys," I say, and I look at Jess.

She looks into her wine and swirls it around.

The thing between me and Jess just started recently. All four of us were drunk, and the boys were playing PlayStation, and me and Jess were in the kitchen, and it just sort of happened. Jess and I were friends in high school—not besties or anything, but we were part of the same circle. It was the kind of friendship that probably would have decayed over time had it not been for social media, but here we are, five years out of high school and still going strong.

When she was fifteen, I gave Jess a ride to an abortion clinic in Philly. It's not like we were that close, but I was the only one in our friend group who had a license. She didn't have a boyfriend at the time, and she didn't tell me who the father was. Didn't tell me much of anything, really, just what I needed to know: her parents couldn't know, and neither could our friends. It was to be a secret that just she and I would share. She fiddled with the strap of her seatbelt the whole way there, and we didn't talk much. Listened to the new Adele and kind of circled around what she was on her way to do. Said things adjacent to but never right on the topic. Things like, "How long do you think it'll take?" and "Do they validate parking?"

It only took about half an hour. When she came back out to the waiting room, her eyes were puffy, but I didn't know if it was from sadness or pain, and I didn't ask. We didn't talk at all on the drive home, except she asked me to stop at the outlets on the way. She needed a new pair of Skechers. All these years later, we've still never talked about it. I don't know if she ever told her parents, told Ryan. Don't know if she plans to have kids. Ryan does, someday, but when the subject comes up, Jess doesn't say much, just kind of nods and shrugs, checks her nail polish for chips.

A few weeks ago, Jess and I were drunk in the kitchen reminiscing about old times. "Remember Kevin Hostetter and how he would carry his drumsticks everywhere?" "You think Miss Grayson was having an affair with Mr. Baldwin?" And then, just like that, we were kissing. Since then, every time the pod gets together, we find an excuse to steal away somewhere and press our lips and bodies against each other. It isn't that I don't love Geoff or that I think marriage is stifling or anything like that. I mean, we haven't even been married a full year. I think we're still figuring it out, this whole sharing your life with another person thing, but it's fine. Marriage is fine. I don't know what it is about Jess. I don't know if it's the boredom or the loneliness or what, but it's the most exciting part of life right now. It's the *only* exciting part of life right now. I think Jess feels the same.

I take a sip and tilt my head back to let the wine settle in my throat before I swallow.

"Uh-oh," Geoff says as red and blue lights stream in through the window. Our townhouse is on a busy street, so it's not like this is unusual. There are cops everywhere around here. Still, no one speaks until the lights disappear down the road.

Ryan breaks the silence. "We could get in major trouble," he says, even though it's not like cops go door to door to check who's in your home. They're not Nazis. "*I* could get in trouble," he adds.

"We should at least be wearing masks," Geoff agrees, but he makes no move to grab one.

"Well, if it weren't for the goddamned mandate," Ryan says.

"No politics." Jess touches Ryan's elbow. He looks angry, but he lets the topic drop and takes a gulp of beer.

"All I know is I can hardly breathe," Jess says. "And they fog up my glasses."

"I'll drink to that," Geoff says and raises his bottle of home-brewed IPA. Geoff always wears his mask, complains incessantly about anti-maskers. But only in private. Only to me.

Jess and Geoff clink bottle to stemless wine glass. "I've tried all kinds of hacks."

"Shaving cream?" I pretend to spray shaving cream into my hand.

"Doesn't work. Dish soap either."

"Here's what I wear." Geoff leans forward and pulls his anti-fog mask out of his back pocket, hands it to Jess.

She turns it over in her hands and shakes her head. "Nothing works. My glasses fog up so bad I can't see."

Geoff and I make eye contact. He won't say anything, not to her. Later, to me, he'll let loose. How much of a Karen she is. How she complains about the most trivial things. But now, in front of the entire group, he stays silent, pulls on his beer and looks away before Jess notices the moment we just shared.

But Jess isn't a Karen, I want to tell him. She can't distinguish her first-world issues from real problems is all. Even so, she's smart—smart enough to know better.

"Oh! We got a cheese and cracker tray," I say. I get up and carry my wine glass into the kitchen.

Jess follows. "Need help?"

I watch over her shoulder as the kitchen door swings closed, and then I set my glass down, place my hands on either side of her face, and kiss her. Her lips soften but don't part. I pull back. "What is it?

She takes a slow sip of wine, then sets her glass on the table. "It's nothing. It's just."

"Ryan?" I look again at the closed door.

She shakes her head.

"I missed you," I say, caressing the top of her hand. "You look absolutely beautiful."

She chews her bottom lip. "I missed you too."

"But," I say. "It's over, isn't it?"

She tilts the palm of her hand up and entwines her fingers with mine. "No."

I give her hand a squeeze.

She releases her hand from mine and lifts her glass to her lips, takes a sip. Finally, she says, "I'm going to leave him."

My stomach twists into a knot, and for a second, I'm pretty sure my heart stops beating. "Yeah?" I ask because I don't know what else to say.

"I already packed a suitcase. I'm leaving in the morning. First thing."

"Where?" I drain the rest of my wine glass, then grab the bottle and refill it.

She shrugs. "A hotel, I guess. Until I figure out where to go next."

I press my palm into the wood grain of the table's surface. "Are you sure?"

She nods. "I've never been more sure of anything." She touches my cheek, kisses me again. "Come with me." It's a statement, not a request.

"Where's that cheese?" It's Geoff, standing in the doorway.

I take a step back, even though it's already too late. He saw how close we were standing. I grab the tray, then pick up my freshly filled wine glass with my free hand. I carry them into the living room, Jess and Geoff following behind me, and set the tray on the coffee table. I sit on the ottoman in front of the easy chair. Geoff takes my old place on the couch, and Jess sits between Geoff and Ryan.

"Thanks, Amanda," Ryan says, leaning over the food tray and building himself a cracker sandwich.

"Thank *you* guys for coming," Geoff answers for me.

Jess is looking at me, but I avoid her gaze and take another sip of wine.

"Did you hear about the Phillies?" Ryan asks Geoff.

I tune out, picture a quiet life in a cottage in Florida, near but not directly by the beach. Saturday mornings, Jess and I'd sit on the front porch drinking southsides and holding hands. I'd say reading, but Jess isn't much of a reader. We like the same shows, though, and both listen to the Killers and Vampire Weekend. It might be nice, that kind of life, where you don't talk current events because she doesn't keep up with the news anyway, and you don't have to bear the weight of a sweaty man with homebrew breath on top of you. No more half-hearted blow jobs. No more backed up bathroom sink after he shaves.

I look at Jess. She is still looking at me. My cheeks burn.

Ryan takes a big bite of his double-decker cracker sandwich, and cracker dust sprays on Jess's lap. She brushes it off.

"You guys are so cute together," I say.

They both look at me like I've said something strange, and I wonder if my words are starting to slur. I'm kind of a lightweight, and I can go from zero to unintelligible in two glasses of wine flat. Including the two I had before Ryan and Jess got here, I'm on my fourth. "I mean it," I say. "You make a good couple."

Jess tilts her head at me, and I look at Ryan and take another sip.

Ryan puts his arm around Jess and draws her to his side. "We have our moments."

"Proof that Tinder isn't just for hookups," Geoff says.

Ryan laughs. "Well, it was *supposed* to be a hookup. But I couldn't get rid of her."

Jess shakes her head. "I would've been fine with a one-night stand, but you wouldn't stop texting me."

Ryan shrugs. "Well, when you know, you know."

"Well, I'll have to let you know about that if I ever find the One," Jess says.

Ryan sighs. "She's been waxing all philosophical about marriage lately. About, like, whether it should exist."

"It's a fair question," I say.

Geoff lifts his eyebrows at me. "Oh? You wish you never married me?"

"Don't get excited," I say. "It *is* kind of a phony thing, vowing to be together forever and all that."

"Exactly," Jess says. "Doesn't really mean you're never going to fall out of love.

"Or get bored with each other," I say.

Jess nods. "And when you do, then what?"

Ryan shakes his head. "For fuck's sake. It's not like we've fallen out of love."

Jess looks down.

"I just wanted to say you're a cute couple," I say. "Didn't mean to stir the pot."

"Jess is just sick of quarantine is all," Ryan says.

I nod, and Geoff nods. Jess takes another sip and says nothing.

"How did you two meet?" Ryan asks. "Don't think I ever heard the story."

"Mutual acquaintance," Geoff says.

"He slid into my DMs," I say.

"She had a boyfriend at the time too," Geoff says.

"You sly dog." Ryan high fives Geoff.

"It was totally fucked up, if you think about it," I say.

"What was?" Geoff asks.

"You pursuing me even though I had a boyfriend. And the fact that I was open to it. Totally fucked up." I try not to look at Jess, but I can see she is looking at me in my periphery.

"Well," Geoff says and shrugs. "He was a dick, anyway."

"That doesn't make it okay," I say.

"In a perfect world, maybe," Jess says. "But things are a lot more complicated, don't you think?"

"Nah, Amanda's right," Ryan says. "Cheating is wrong. No matter the situation."

"But they ended up together," Jess says, motioning to me, then Geoff. "It wasn't just a meaningless fling."

"Doesn't matter," Ryan says.

"Yeah," I say. "Some things are just wrong. Cheating on your spouse is wrong."

Jess taps her fingernails against her wine glass. "Your boyfriend."

"Right," I say. "Yeah. That's what I meant. Cheating on your boyfriend is wrong."

"Cheery topic for a Saturday night," Ryan says.

"Cheating is always wrong," Geoff says. The way he looks at me makes my stomach turn cold. He's kind of squinting, and though his lips curve into a smile, the smile doesn't reach his eyes.

My pulse beats in my ears. I look from Geoff to Jess, and they blur together into one amorphous form. I open my mouth to speak, but nothing comes out, and I think I'm going to be sick. I stand up unsteadily, race toward the bathroom, reach the toilet just in time. Geoff calls out to me, "You okay?" I drop my forehead to the cool porcelain.

"You good?" This time it's Jess. She's kneeling in the doorway of the bathroom and reaching out to pull my hair back.

"Yes," I mumble. "I'm good. I'm good." I close my eyes and listen to my own breathing. It sounds like waves crashing against the beach. "I'm good," I say one more time and try my best to believe it.

It isn't until the next afternoon that we find out Jess has gone missing. She isn't there when Ryan gets home from work, and her side of the closet has been cleared out. "She didn't even leave a note," Ryan texts Geoff. "Thought maybe she was with you guys."

Do I know where she's gone, Geoff wants to know. "You must," he says. "She must have told you."

But I don't have any idea where she could be, and it bothers me that I don't. "It's not like we're that close," I tell Geoff, and later, Ryan, when he stops by.

"Then text her and ask," Ryan says.

"I don't even know if she'd respond," I try.

"She will." Ryan looms over me, still in his uniform, and for the first time I'm aware how tall he is, well over 6 feet. How commanding his presence. I wonder what it must feel like to be on the other end of a confrontation with him. Wonder if he's ever used force against a suspect.

"Amanda," Ryan pleads, "you're her best friend. She trusts you. Please."

"Do it," Geoff says. "She'll respond to you."

I pull out my phone and stare at it for a second before I type, "Did you do it?" The wait for a reply is excruciating. Geoff and Ryan are both watching me watch my phone. My hands feel clammy.

Finally, three little dots appear, and then a message. "Yes," she says, and then, "I'm at the Mason. Room 115." A third message comes through within seconds: "I'm pregnant. Don't tell Geoff."

Before I can even process what I just read, Ryan snatches the phone from me. "What the fuck?" He presses the phone back into my hands. "She's been drinking."

"Ryan," I say, but he's already on his way out the door. "Fuck," I say, and type out a quick warning to Jess: "Ryan knows. I'm sorry. Think he's on his way to the hotel."

"What just happened?" Geoff asks.

"She's," I say, but my mouth feels dry and I can't push the word out.

"Did you tell her he's coming?"

I don't answer.

"What the fuck, Amanda? This is none of our business."

"She has a right to leave if she wants," I say.

"He has a right to an explanation." Geoff's voice is clipped, heated.

"She doesn't owe him anything," I say, but it isn't true, and I know it.

He laughs, but it's an angry laugh. Mean. "She married him, didn't she? You don't just leave like that. You don't just-" he waves his right hand in the air, "step out."

I look down at my phone again. Three dots appear on Jess's side of the screen, but then they disappear again. I look back up at Geoff. He's watching me.

"You don't know how she might be feeling," I say.

"You don't know how *he* feels."

"No," I agree. "But. Maybe it's not about him."

"Then what's it about?" Geoff asks.

"Maybe it's about lockdown," I say. "Maybe it's about the whole world crumbling and dying around us, and we can't even shake hands or hug or just, I don't know, smile anymore because no one can see that you're smiling anyway. Maybe she's sick of only seeing his face and she's wondering why, of all the faces in all the world, this is the only one she gets to see. Maybe she just wants it all to be over."

"The pandemic?" he asks.

I shrug. Silence fills the space between us for a moment.

Then finally, he asks, "What did I do?" His voice is calmer now, defeated.

"You didn't do anything," I say. "It's not anything."

"Then," he says, twisting his hands in and out of each other. "Then why?"

I open my mouth, but there is no answer, and my phone begins to sing. I look down, expecting Jess, but it's my sister on Facetime. Geoff looks at me, waiting. He thinks it is Jess, too. I answer. My niece's left eye and half her forehead fill my screen. "Aunt Manda," she says. Her words spill out of her mouth so quickly, I have to replay them in my head to understand: "You never told me how the story ends." She holds a picture book up to the camera, too close. I can just make out the image of a princess on the cover.

"Oh," I say. "I forgot."

"You forgot how it ends?" she asks.

I look at Geoff. He cocks his head at me, lifts an eyebrow.

"I'm a little busy right now, Michelle. Can I call you later?"

"But how does it end?"

"All stories end the same, don't they?"

"Happily ever after," she says.

It isn't the ending I had in mind, but I like her ending more than my own, so I nod and force a smile. "That's right," I say, because some lies need telling. "Happily ever after. That's how all stories end."

THE FINAL SCORE

The game began forty-seven years ago. John, in his crumpled slacks after a long day at the office, sat cross-legged on the stained carpet across from Mary, nothing between them but cards. They could only play a few hands before John Jr. would notice they weren't paying attention to him, would begin banging his teething ring against the plastic edge of his playpen like a prisoner in an old movie. But a few hands at a time was better than nothing. Originally, they'd agreed they'd play to five hundred, but when Mary reached the target so quickly—after just three days—they extended the objective to a thousand, then five.

It became a sort of running joke: a winner would be declared only when one of them passed away. There was a period of about two years—in their early forties—when John was several thousand points ahead, but Mary caught up to him, even passed him for a while. And so it went for years and years, John would be ahead, then Mary, then John. The game kept going and going, through it all. Through John Jr.'s childhood, his graduation, his marriage; through John's infidelity, apology, penance;

through Mary's illness, then her remission; through John's illness, his stay at the hospital, his hospice days back home.

The winner, it turned out, was John. Mary checked the score scratched on the scrap paper before folding it up and sliding it inside the card box. Afterward, she wasn't sure what to do with the cards. In the end, she gave them to John Jr., who'd grown up watching his parents play the game. When she told him she was giving the cards to him, he protested, but only a little.

"I can't take them," John Jr. said, even as he reached out for the box. "You should keep them."

Mary shrugged. "What am I going to do with them? The game is over," she said. "I lost."

With the game over, the evenings seemed longer. Mary took up knitting, but it didn't stick. She moved in with John Jr. and learned to play cribbage. She'd play most evenings with John Jr.'s wife, Marina, but it wasn't the same. Mary missed the continuous nature of the old game with John, the illusion that the game would go on forever, that there would always be time to even the score.

Years later, after his mother was long gone, after Marina was long gone too—happily remarried to a dentist in Lancaster, and with two kids, neither one John Jr.'s doing—John Jr. came upon the old deck of cards while trying to make room in his closet for his new live-in girlfriend. He didn't remember those early days, when his parents played on the porch while he distracted himself watching ants. He didn't remember the later days, much, either. He was preoccupied with his own life back then—a pre-teen, then a teen, then a college student, and then, and then. The game's title was faded, almost unreadable, and the once stiff box had softened and torn. The cards felt light in his hands, and without much thought, he tossed the worn box into the large trash bag with the rest of the clutter he didn't know what to do with.

ACKNOWLEDGEMENTS

First and foremost, thanks to Barrett Warner for taking a chance and spending the time to help me learn and grow as a writer. It goes without saying that this collection wouldn't be what it is without your careful feedback, and I wouldn't be the writer I am (and am still becoming) without your guidance.

Thanks, also, to the many people who have given me feedback on drafts of these stories, especially Justus Humphrey, Jen Hirt, Cat Rios, Bernadette Lear, Maggie Gerrity, Eric Bliman, and Heather Hamilton. Thanks, also, to the Catapult workshop led by the brilliant Ploi Pirapokin, who helped me step out of my comfort zone and write from the perspective of a chicken.

Thanks to the Boppers, who celebrated with me every time one of these stories was accepted for publication, and whose friendship is one of my favorite things about life.

And thanks, as always, to Damien Munoz Cowger, for your feedback and companionship all these years. Here's to many more!

And thanks to Maxy. I love you so much, kiddo. May these stories encourage you to continue creating your own.

Stories in this collection were previously published (sometimes in slightly different form) in the following:

How to Figure the Returns appeared in *The Santa Clara Review*.

Thirty-Eight Today appeared in *Prime Number Magazine*.

Better Days appeared in *Fleas on the Dog* with the title Fifty-Four Minutes.

Thank You and God Bless appeared in *Free State Review*.

First Snow appeared in *Jabberwock Review* with the title After the First Snow.

Bubble appeared in *Parhelion Literary Magazine*.

The Final Score appeared in *The Lindenwood Review*.

ABOUT ASHLEY COWGER

Ashley Cowger (she/they) is the author of two short story collections: *On the Plus Side* (Galileo Press) and *Peter Never Came* (Autumn House Press). Their fiction and creative nonfiction have appeared in several literary journals. They teach English at Penn State Harrisburg.

www.ingramcontent.com/pod-product-compliance
Lightning Source LLC
Chambersburg PA
CBHW030412120726
47904CB00007B/2240